# Introduction: Thirteen Moons over Vietnam

*Thirteen Moons over Vietnam* is a thirteen-volume series revealing the moral and emotional trials of a military policeman in the Vietnam War. Ben Thieu Long (a pseudonym) struggled to maintain his bearings in a minefield of temptations and ethical contradictions. His behavior swung like a pendulum across contrasting moral choices. As a policeman trained to enforce laws, he crossed lines, blurring the distinction between law enforcer and lawbreaker. Expected to obey military rules of engagement, he vacillated between a hesitant pacifist and an intense aggressor.

These stories illustrate the turmoil one soldier felt as he encountered moral contradictions in war, resulting in a spiritual crisis that weakened Ben's adherence to his values and faith. Raised as a devout Christian with a strict moral standard, he ricocheted between his values and the dark seduction of temptation. How well he recognized his limitations, employed resources to sustain his faith, and weathered the journey is one soldier's story, while reflecting a pattern that related to countless veterans across generations.

## Personal Tribulations and Life-long Consequences

Even morally strong people misstep in the face of tempting circumstances. Some choices have profound effects, resulting in scars for life. Behaviors in response to fear and social pressure may torment a person's conscience, mocking their expectations and shredding their self-concept. Some individuals face a crossroad that poses diverging paths with serious implications for their sense of self-worth, purpose, and character. Traumatic experiences shatter a person's beliefs.

Soldiers in war may encounter ethical choices, and moral lines are blurred when they choose safety or impulsive emotions over moral behavior. Subsequently, soldiers may compartmentalize their experiences as a mechanism for self-preservation, concealing truth, and protecting their self-image. This pattern, prolonged under stress, may continue for years after their military service.

## From Innocence to Temptation to Remorse

### 1ST MOON: INNOCENCE ~ RECAP

We met Ben in his initial month in Vietnam when he arrived as a loving husband but naïve soldier. Before his tour, he had focused on reinforcing the relationship with his wife, strengthening his faith, and fortifying his ability to handle whatever may lie ahead. He was determined to adhere to his values and avoid falling into temptations.

Ben's ability to manage his behavior began to fracture as temptations of drugs, alcohol, and women presented a distraction from the war. He sensed that different responses would be needed to cope in his new environment. He tried to shield himself from emotional vulnerability, but it wasn't evident whether these behaviors were temporary adjustments or a shift toward a different approach to life.

### 2ND MOON: TEMPTATION ~ RECAP

Ben's second month presented a gauntlet of temptations. Drugs and women provided escapism, and opportunities to enhance wealth and power became addictive activities. Each choice brought its consequences. His foray into temptation ruptured his sense of morality and tore at his spiritual fabric. The tension between what was right and how he behaved fueled an internal struggle; he was losing the battle to adhere to his values and commitments. A destructive metamorphosis was overpowering him.

## 3ᴿᴰ MOON: DISCORD ~ RECAP

Ben's third month continued his spiral into the darker aspects of behavior. The birth of his child late in his second month, coupled with frequent incidents of moral failures, began to weigh on his well-being. A mood of discord and doom deepened as his behavior moved farther from his core values.

## 4ᵀᴴ MOON: REMORSE ~ RECAP

Ben's fourth month triggered a personal crisis regarding betrayal of his values as he moved deeper into the darkest aspects of Saigon's criminal environment. Ben faced a pivotal decision about his future, and embarked on a different path, in hopes of escaping the moral temptations that had drawn him from his core values.

5th *Moon: Insights* is next in the series, and we follow Ben as he has transferred to a new company focused on highway patrol duty. He will encounter a new set of challenges, including unsettling experiences of death, dismay, and new temptations. Ben also learns an unexpected lesson on trust and distrust. These experiences lead to greater insights into the character of leaders, coping with death, and deepening his understanding about priorities in life and the importance of strengthening character in the face of challenges.

*Saigon – Long Binh Hwy Static Posts*

# LEADERS' TALK: Follow Me!

## April 1, 1970

### Meet the New Boss

Ben and the other MPs who transferred to their new MP Company completed their cross-training orientation. They learned from seasoned MPs how to effectively patrol the highway and now assumed full responsibility for their new duties.

They filed into the hooch to meet the new leaders for their fully manned MP Company. The assembly required all three platoons to attend. The building measured eighty feet long, wide enough for two rows of metal bunks and a six-foot-wide center aisle, and housed twenty men.

Ben stepped inside with Greg Pulaski and Tucker Bronson. "Wow, it's crowded in here," he whispered. "There are more guys in our company than I realized."

Tucker nodded. "Must be over a hundred of us. We're triple-packed in here for this meet-and-greet show."

"I'm looking forward to finding out whether I'll be assigned to highway day patrol or night convoy duty," Greg stated.

"I wonder how we'll like our new Sergeants? I hope they aren't like those two we had at Pershing," Ben added.

"You mean Denton and his suck-up friend?" Tucker asked. "No shit! I bet you don't want that again!"

One of the E-7s snapped, interrupting all conversations. "Heads up, gentlemen! We're not at a high school dance."

Everyone immediately fell silent.

The E-7 continued, "Our new Platoon Sergeants have arrived. The purpose of this orientation is to meet them. Most of you are new to this company, and since no one knows anyone else, that'll be a fresh start for everyone."

Ben glanced around and noted that nearly everyone was a stranger. He and Greg exchanged glances and grinned but remained silent.

"Now, most of you have been in the Army long enough to know how much we like order and routine." The E-7 paused as if he'd said something profound, then continued, "However, nothing is routine about our circumstances. Command has fully re-manned this company, drawing from Three Corp." (Designation for the area north of the Delta and south of the Central Highlands).

The E-7 paused to study the faces of the men. "This is very unusual for the military because we never throw men together into a unit where everyone's new to the situation. That means we face a unique challenge because we won't have soldiers with the knowledge gained by actually performing the duty for months. We'll lose that experience when our trainers depart for their next duty station."

Mumbling rippled throughout the assembly as several men nodded.

Although the hooch was full, Ben noticed a few men missing – eighteen on highway patrol duty and an equal number from another platoon. *They're probably racked out after pulling convoy duty all night.*

"ATTEN-SHUN!" the E-7 barked as the MPC Captain entered the room.

"At ease," the Captain ordered. "All right, men, listen up. We're taking over our AO tomorrow. This meeting is to introduce two new E-6 Platoon Sergeants. You'll be assigned to one of them today, but it's important to meet both."

The Sergeants entered and stood behind the Captain. A stillness hung over the gathering as the men looked them over.

Tucker whispered, "Meet the new boss, same as the old boss."

The Captain continued, "First up is Sergeant Rockwell. He will lead the 1st Platoon that's responsible for Night Overtake, the convoy escort duty. Following Rockwell, we will hear from Sergeant Simon, who will lead the 2nd Platoon for the day shift's Highway Patrol duty. Both men bring strong leadership skills."

Without asking for comments, the Captain turned to Sergeant Rockwell. "Take over, Sergeant Rockwell."

## You'll Like Me

Sergeant Rockwell stood tall at six feet four inches. His round face with chubby cheeks and horn-rimmed glasses made him look more like a professor than an intimidating MP.

"Good morning, men. I'm Staff Sergeant Rockwell," he softly announced.

"He doesn't sound tough to me," Tucker mumbled to Ben. They were in the back of the hooch so the Captain and Sergeant couldn't hear the ripple of chuckles from men reacting to the sarcastic remark.

Sergeant Rockwell continued, "I'm new in-country, but I have a lot of MP experience, including two Stateside and one duty station in Germany. I'm a graduate of Fort Gordon's MP School, so I received the same training."

Someone on a footlocker next to Ben turned and loudly pro-claimed, "Oh fuck, this guy's a cherry!" Mumbling and nervous twitching rippled throughout the hooch. *Shit! Our new convoy escort leader has only just arrived in-country!*

The Sergeant overheard the remark and added, "I'm new, but I've had an excellent orientation to the operations of this company. Don't be concerned about my readiness. I'm a fast learner and expect that we'll get off to a strong start with Night Overtake."

Ben carefully examined Sergeant Rockwell. He appeared plump in a uniform that hung unevenly. His fatigue shirt bulged slightly at the waist, and his trousers were rumpled. *His appearance seems off, but maybe my initial impression is too harsh? But Military Police are perfectionists about dress code and uniform violations. If this guy's such a professional, why is he so sloppy? Maybe he just landed and hasn't had time to get his fatigues starched.*

He whispered to Tucker, "Does he look out of shape?"

"Yeah, I was wondering about that. Maybe this guy's been riding a desk instead of running patrols."

The soldier on the footlocker added, "Running convoy isn't light duty. If this guy's a desk jockey, we're in for trouble. We've got to be fast and tough out there."

Sergeant Rockwell's declaration interrupted their conversation. "I'd like to share my philosophy on leadership. I'm a fair and posi-tive leader. I respect you and want to maintain a good relationship with everyone. You can come to me with any issues. I'm open and accessible."

"Now he sounds like one of those hippies," the seated MP snort-ed. "I suppose next we'll have a love-in and sing Kumbaya."

"I don't know," Ben argued. "He sounds positive to me. It'd be nice to have a decent Platoon Sergeant instead of an overbearing jerk."

"Don't be so naive! There are no decent Sergeants. We're not on a college campus – this is Vietnam! This guy's all wrong. Either he's lying, or he has no clue how to lead men. I bet this is his first platoon leadership assignment. Just listen to him! This is bullshit, and it won't work."

Ben took a deep breath. "The Army has too many old-school Sergeants, but he sounds like a good one. Maybe he's decent. We need more leaders who show respect and openness. I'd be okay being in his platoon."

Sergeant Rockwell continued, "I'm sure you're going to like being in my platoon. I'm a good leader, I'm easy to work for, and we'll have a good time." He paused, folded his arms, and grinned while surveying the crowd.

"He's pretty full of himself, isn't he?" the footlocker MP sniped. "Sure sounds like we'd be lucky to be in his platoon, him being a wonderful leader and all." He turned to see who agreed with him, and several guys nodded.

Ben didn't want to argue or draw additional attention. *Why do these guys have such a negative attitude toward him? Sergeant Rockwell sounds positive. He's probably a good leader. How could anyone not want to be in his platoon?*

The footlocker MP continued to criticize. "He's no Sergeant Rock, and he's not even a manly looking dude. This guy's got a misleading name."

The same men in the back of the hooch nodded again, and the footlocker MP rocked back and forth with a wide grin.

The Captain asked if anyone had a question.

Ben listened to the Sergeant's direct responses to various questions. *Rockwell seems to be who he says he is. His answers are open and positive. Everyone should appreciate the opportunity to work for him. Some of the guys seem cynical. Why can't they take him at face value and respect what he says? Their attitude doesn't seem fair.*

The Captain thanked Sergeant Rockwell.

## I'll Make You Tough

Sergeant Simon stepped forward to address the assembly. He was also an E-6 but shorter and thinner, with a weathered face *Man, he doesn't even smile like Sergeant Rockwell does. I don't like this guy!*

"I'm from an infantry division and proud of it!" the Sergeant snapped. "I've been in-country eight months, most of it in the field. I've recently cross-trained as an MP, but that's not my claim to fame. I'm a natural leader. My motto is *Follow Me*, and I've got the experience and skills to lead you."

Again the footlocker MP offered an opinion. "Well, this one's a piece of work, isn't he? Not even a professional MP but so cocky that he thinks he's a natural leader who can move us forward. What an ass!"

Sergeant Simon glared in their direction. "Now, some of you might have a problem with that."

The Sergeant couldn't have overheard that remark, but he seemed to read body language. "I don't need to know every job to be a strong leader. My approach is to understand the mission and properly use people. Don't worry if I didn't go to school. I've learned more in the real world than they teach in school."

Several in the crowd mumbled when the confident Sergeant implied he was smarter than any of them. The footlocker MP rocked sideways to comment, but Sergeant Simon caught his movement. He leaned behind Ben and kept quiet.

Sergeant Simon directly challenged the rumblings. "I understand what our assignment requires. My style is to ensure mission integrity. That means my orders rule, and everyone *will* learn and fulfill *their* duty."

He scanned the group for reactions, but no one stirred. The Sergeant's piercing glare felt like a spotlight focused on them.

He resumed his introduction. "I expect everyone to follow orders.

You will report at formation on time and ready. I won't tolerate slackers or half-assed efforts. Nobody in my unit will jog. We always move at full speed."

Ben and the other MPs fell eerily silent. Only the sound of passing traffic filled the room. *We're not used to receiving such an ass-chewing from an outsider! Simon's manner is similar to how we confront GIs. We're not usually on the receiving end, especially by an infantry guy. He has a lot of nerve talking to seasoned MPs like this!*

He examined Sergeant Simon and noticed his fatigues were pressed and starched and hung stiff. *That's impressive! He pays more attention to the dress code and uniform detail than Rockwell.*

Sergeant Simon continued, "I've made my expectations clear. Now I want to make my reasoning clear. I'm a hard leader. I've seen men die because they weren't prepared or focused. My approach isn't because I enjoy fucking with them; it's because I'm responsible for their lives. Nobody wants anyone in their command to be hurt or killed. No leader wants that guilt on his conscience."

Again the Sergeant scanned the room for reactions. Everyone's attention focused intently on him in silence. Ben responded to his commanding presence. He hesitated to turn his head or whisper for fear of the consequences.

Sergeant Simon added, "If anyone fucks up or fails to demonstrate total focus to the mission, I'll ride their ass and put a world of hurt on them. Nobody—no-fucking-body—in my platoon will be anything other than squared away and top quality. I'll not tolerate soldiers who aren't hard-charging all the time. If they don't perform at a consistently high level, they'll find I'm their worst nightmare, and they'll be crying for their mamas."

Feeling in full command of the group, the Sergeant concluded his talk. "If you work for me, I'll make you tough. You'll be hard as nails. No one will look at you and think they can take you down. Of course, no one will like you either. But you have two choices over here, and now you're getting my eight months of experience in Nam. You can be nice and get dead or be a prick. I intend to make every one of you a bad-ass and a tough MP. That will make you a reliable, solid partner and help ensure that we all go home safe."

He paused again. The men could hear a pin drop; it didn't seem like they were even breathing.

"Make no mistake about it – I'm a leader because I deliver results. In my platoon, it will be my way, all the way, all the time. No second opinions, no second options."

Not once during the talk did Ben see a glimmer of a smile from Sergeant Simon. He was all business, bordering on angry and mean. *I'm not sure what drives this guy, but he sure is intimidating. I certainly don't want to be in his platoon. There'd be too high a risk of screwing up and getting messed over. I can't tell what others are thinking, but I'll bet most guys who've heard these two leaders prefer Sergeant Rockwell.*

## Hearts and Minds

The Captain stepped forward and announced, "All right, men. Check the company bulletin board for the platoon rosters. Dismissed." He and the Sergeants exited the hooch.

Clusters of men gathered to talk over what they just heard. The mid-morning temperature had risen to eighty-four degrees. "The EM Club is air-conditioned; let's get out of the heat," one of them suggested.

Ben walked out of the hooch when someone called to him. "Hey, why don't you join us? We're going to the EM Club."

He recognized the guy from the footlocker. "Me?"

"Yes, Long, I'm talking to you. Who the fuck do you think I'm talking to?" he responded sarcastically. "You were offering your opinion. Might as well see this conversation through, don't you think?"

Ben was taken aback by his aggressiveness but agreed. "Okay, just let me check the bulletin board. I want to know where I'm landing."

"Just don't duck out on us. Come over to the EM Club once you figure that out. We may be working together."

"Sure, I'll be there," Ben replied. He felt intimidated by the man's bluntness, not sure whether that guy already knew the assignments.

Ben headed toward the bulletin board. *I still can't believe how well we lucked out with these facilities. This base is surreal, not like anything I'd ever expect to find here. We have real concrete sidewalks, perfectly edged and notched, just like in the real world. We only had wood-slatted walkways at Pershing Field.*

The Sergeants' speeches spiked everyone's interest in knowing their assignments. A dozen guys already huddled around the bulletin board. Ben waited to read the duty roster, leaning forward to listen to the various opinions. Contrasting perceptions favored neither Sergeant. Men assigned to the same platoon argued about whether their new platoon leader would be good or bad news.

"I like Rockwell," one soldier emphatically stated. "He sounds like a good guy."

"He looks like a loser; I don't think he has the experience to do the job," another challenged. "I wouldn't follow him into a whorehouse, let alone trust him to lead our convoy escort team."

"He's better than that arrogant Simon," a third man insisted.

"But Simon's got combat experience, and with eight months incountry, he's probably got his shit together. That's a big deal," a fourth man countered.

Ben moved forward to search the lists for his name. He didn't find his name on the first roster and stepped sideways to examine the next one.

"Oh shit," he mumbled when he found SP4 Long printed on the second platoon roster.

"At least you have a real soldier for a leader," a nearby MP offered.

Another MP chimed in, "Too bad! He's an overbearing prick and will make your life a living hell. I lucked out and got the decent Sergeant in the 1st Platoon."

Ben felt torn by the contrary comments and stepped back. *I prefer the friendly Sergeant, not the strict, wrapped-too-tight infantry wanna-be MP.*

He briskly walked past another group discussing their assignments and the possible implications. *There's so much disagreement I wonder if any good will come out of this Meet Your New Leaders meeting. Wasn't the whole idea to bring clarity about our platoon leaders? Instead, it's the opposite effect. Men are conflicted about the new Sergeants' qualifications and character.*

Ben stepped into the EM Club, and the cold air and darkness hit him like a double punch. He leaned against the wall until his eyes adjusted, enjoying the refreshing coolness. The club was full and abuzz with animated conversations. A soldier waved from the left, and he recognized the guy from the footlocker.

"Hello, Long, I'm Frank Succors. I know you're from Saigon. You don't know me, but I was in the 1st Platoon on the opposite shift."

"Oh," Ben stammered, embarrassed he didn't recognize him.

"Never mind, meet your new partners. We're all 2nd Platoon." Frank introduced the other five MPs at the table, including Greg and Tucker. "We figured we better band together if we're going to survive working for Sergeant Simon. He's not a real MP, and he's a prick. We professionals must stay tight. What we want to know is where do you stand?"

Ben was taken aback by Frank's brashness and fumbled for words as the five men stared at him. "It is what it is. I was hoping for Rockwell because he has the MP school background, but we've drawn the short straw, and Sergeant Simon's our platoon leader. I don't know what to think, but I'm afraid this will get ugly fast if we don't meet his expectations."

One of the other MPs added, "Yeah, and given he's infantry and not a professional MP, how can he set reasonable expectations?"

Frank nodded and elaborated, "We need to figure out how to play this. If we work together, our chances are a lot better."

Ben was unclear about the group's objective. "A lot better for what? What're you thinking? The Sergeant calls the shots. What else is there to do?"

"Simon showed his style!" Tucker declared. "He expects us to toe the line right away. He made that very clear. But once we leave guard mount and get on the highway, we're in a different world. He can't be everywhere."

"You know those speeches are hearts-and-minds crap," Frank clarified. "Leaders try to win your hearts with talk to appeal to your values and seduce your mind so you'll fall in line and follow them. They're playing games. He's throwing bullshit, expecting us to eat it up and blindly follow him."

"What do you want from me?" Ben asked.

"Nothing, we just want to know how you interpreted Simon's talk and what your attitude is about all of this," Frank replied.

"As I said, his style worries me, but I don't want trouble because I ignored his signals."

"Nobody wants trouble, man, but nobody wants to be fucked over either," Tucker asserted. "You've got to know who your friends are and who you can trust. The highway is no place to be without backup."

"Yes, we share the same goal, to be safe and know our partners have our back."

"Good! Let's drink to teamwork," Greg announced and lifted his beer toward the center of the table, signaling a toast.

Ben worried about social pressure and decided to go along to get along for the time being. *The last thing we all need is conflict in the ranks! The one thing we all agree on is staying safe and getting home in one piece.*

## Letter Home 122: *April 2, 1970; 1000 hours*

*Dearest Love:*

*I am hard pressed for time here and don't get any days off so don't be upset if I don't write but once or twice a week. My heart is with you.*

*I like the work I am doing because it is far from boring.*

*I meet new people and situations every time I go out on the highway.*

*My nose and chin and cheeks are sunburned and peeling.*

*The monsoon season has started, last night it poured so heavy that the barracks next door flooded. Ha ha. I had just moved out that afternoon – looks like life is still going my way.*

*I love you so much my darling, I wish we could be together now but sometimes life is unreasonable. I really miss my Aphrodite, running her hands through my hair and cooing in my ear.*

*I got the medal you sent, thank you very much. It means as much to me as it does to you.*

*P.S. I'm doing patrol logs now, and required to write all my entries with military time (2400 clock). To keep my mind consistent, I'll now date and time all my letters in military time too.*

*I love you forever,*

*Ben*

# RAISED TO TRUST: Beliefs

## April 4, 1970

### Foundations of Trust

Ben rummaged through his footlocker for paper. *There's hardly anyone here right now, so I'm going to write a letter. It's not often this place is so quiet.*

A voice from behind interrupted his search for a pen. "I'm surprised to find you here. It looks like everyone else is gone."

Ben turned to see Randy DeMarco a few feet away. "Yeah, it's like a ghost town in here. Shift change is the low ebb of the day, you know. Most guys are either still on the highway or at guard mount for the night convoy. Those who aren't on duty probably have gone to the club. It's a big day because of the new Sergeants and our platoon assignments."

Randy glanced toward the end of the hooch, where he saw two soldiers hunched over a chessboard. "Looks like the smart kids stayed behind."

Ben laughed, "Yeah, life can be lonely when you don't have a vice to keep you occupied."

"I didn't think you were one of the unfortunate guys who didn't have a vice," Randy mocked.

Ben smiled as he dropped his papers into the footlocker. "I'm not suffering. I've got plenty of vices. But it's been a crazy day, and I need to sort things out."

"I heard talk about the new Platoon Sergeants."

"Yeah, it was weird. By the way, where were you? I didn't see your name on the duty roster, so I expected you'd have been there."

"Sick call, man. I got a nasty rash on my foot, and it itches like crazy. I can show you if you want to see it."

Ben waved his hand. "No, thanks. I'll take your word for it."

"Don't worry; they gave me an ointment. The doc said it should go away in a week or two."

"Keep your itchy feet off my bunk until then," Ben ordered.

"Talk about an itch; what's got you so irritated?"

Ben sat on his footlocker and explained, "This morning, the new E-6s gave their introductions, and I was surprised by the reactions. Some guys aren't willing to accept the new Sergeants at their word and trust them, even though we've just met them."

"Really? Do they think the Sergeants were blowing smoke out their ass?"

"I don't know. Some of the guys said the talk was all bullshit."

"What about you?"

"They sounded straight to me. I was taught to trust people, so I'm gonna take a guy at his word."

"That's good for you, but people aren't all raised the same."

Ben frowned and continued, "I was taught to respect and accept others. That's a cornerstone of my Christian Baptist upbringing."

"I get it. My background is similar, although from a different church."

"Some people believe there are big differences between the churches, but I think most share the same values."

"But there still can be important differences."

Ben added, "I was a Boy Scout, and that shaped my values and behavior."

"How so?"

"Boy Scouts emphasized you do your best to do your duty to God and country. My commitment motivated me to earn the God and Country Award. I believe our leaders are trustworthy. When a leader says something, I trust that he or she is truthful."

"We share that belief too. My parents raised me to believe that our leaders had our best interests at heart."

Ben added, "And I thought other people were raised the same. That's how it was where I grew up. That's why I'm surprised guys are so quick to be negative."

"I get that you're disappointed some men don't trust the new Sergeants, but being a leader doesn't mean they're perfect. Leaders do have faults."

"I feel it's going too far to automatically distrust all leaders without giving them a chance to prove themselves. It's judging them without giving them a chance to show they're good people. That's not fair," Ben insisted.

## Trust your Government

Randy shook his head. "We're living in controversial times; attitudes are changing."

"I thought Americans viewed the government and business leaders positively in the '50s. Eisenhower was loved and trusted by my parents' generation."

"It wasn't all roses then either. There was a lot of distrust that arose from the McCarthy campaign to call out communists in our country."

"I'm not familiar with all that. All I know is we hate Communists. After all, isn't that why we're here in Vietnam—to fight Communism?"

"That's what they've told us. But sometimes life's complicated, and there are different explanations for why some things happen. I mean, look what's been happening the past few years. There've been assassinations, race riots, and the war in Vietnam, and that's just the headlines."

"There's a lot of turmoil, that's for sure," Ben sighed.

"And that turmoil, with some people thinking differently about why it's happening, has increased suspicion about leaders' intentions. That's why there's less confidence in leaders and a general tendency to question authority."

"I'm torn about some of that too, but I still believe we should give people the benefit of the doubt."

"And that makes sense where you come from, but the benefit of the doubt has been disappearing for other people," Randy replied. "If you don't know it, the benefit of the doubt has never been an attitude for some people—like Blacks or Indians. They've had distrust issues from the get-go, and those are justifiable."

"I'm aware of race riots in some of the bigger cities and the increase in anti-war protests," Ben acknowledged. "Resentment seems to be on the rise!"

"I grew up in Detroit and can tell you that Blacks haven't had much reason to trust the police or the government. And all of the recent anti-war protests indicate that a whole lot of white people are also losing trust in leaders and the government."

"I've lived in a small town since I was nine, and everyone there seemed to be patriotic. Neighbors came out to wave flags at holiday parades."

"Small towns are probably still like that, but attitudes in big cities are changing. Maybe that's why we see friction in our ranks between guys from small towns and big cities. They think differently and don't mix well," Randy observed.

"I've experienced that friction. There's a disagreement about whether we're fighting the spread of Communism or if we are throwing poor people into a war that provides profit for the military-industrial complex."

"That's the argument between the patriotic right and the anti-war protesters. Those divisions are popping up in more and more places, including within our own ranks."

"Yep, it's like the saying – my country, love it or leave it!" Ben exclaimed.

"Trust in our government hasn't been this divided since the Civil War. There's a political war at home about why we're fighting in Vietnam."

Ben nodded. "Trust in the government is lower than it used to be."

"And that attitude of distrust is spreading."

## Military Culture

"But people's distrust of the government shouldn't create problems in the military. Our training requires us to follow orders and respect our officers and NCOs," Ben argued. "Non-commissioned officers or Sergeants need to be obeyed too. Our ability to do our duty and return home safely depends on trusting those around us—and above us."

Randy added, "But that's changing too. Hostile attitudes and insubordinate behavior is increasing, especially among draftees in the lower ranks."

Ben thought of Brad Morrison and his non-regulation hippie glasses.

Randy added, "Maybe they got that attitude because they've on the lower rungs of our great society. Draftees are guys who didn't go to college or couldn't afford to pay a doctor to get a bogus 'unfit for duty' excuse to avoid the military."

"I'll agree that being less advantaged increases your chances of being drafted. The draft board moved fast to scoop me up when I lost my college deferment."

"Exactly!"

Ben continued, increasingly frustrated, "It looks like the guys who volunteer are more patriotic and stronger supporters of the war and government. The RAs *chose* to join the military. They're committed to defending our country by fighting Communism."

"Yes, and all that fuels more friction. Our society is becoming more divided about whether to believe in the integrity of leaders or not to trust anything."

Ben paused and asked, "I wonder how this would play at the EM Club?"

## Implications of Distrust

Randy shook his head. "I'm worried about the impact these changing attitudes have on men in the field, and particularly for us as we patrol the highways. Disagreements could turn ugly and affect compliance to orders, or at least how willing guys are to back each other up. That type of disunity could bring danger to guys who don't get support from the men around them."

Ben's brow furrowed. "You don't believe that, do you?"

"I wish I didn't, but how can you not wonder? When men have such strong disagreements that they don't trust each other, the next step is to pull away and not take risks. That means guys won't put themselves at risk to help others. That puts men in danger, whether among the police or in the infantry."

"That destroys the power and effectiveness of a team too. I don't even want to imagine that behavior happening!"

"It would be our worst nightmare, that's for sure."

"So who we work with could be a matter of life or death or at least safety versus the risk of danger," Ben responded in a low tone.

"In the worst-case scenario, yes. Trust has never been more important."

**Letter Home 123:** *April 6, 1970; 0730 hours*

*My Darling Sue:*

*I got the Easter card and letter marked pages 45 to 78.*

*I may not be able to answer everything, but I'll do my best.*

*All my love,*

*Ben*

## **Letter Home 124:** *April 8, 1970; 2000 hours*

*Dearest Sue:*

*As you can see time flies here.*

*I've gotten a couple more letters and I'm so sorry for what I've done to you. Please forgive me my darling. I did not mean to imply like you were anything like your mother and I'm sorry you read it that way. I guess I'm losing my ability to communicate in letters.*

*Please keep sending your love, I need it more than anything else. I may never get a chance to call so don't get upset if I don't.*

*I'm having problems here merely because I'm so lonesome for some intelligent people. There is no one to talk to and no one to love here.*

*I do love you, Sue, and 12,000 miles is nothing to my heart.*

*I'm not cracking up because I've passed the crisis over the last two or three weeks, but I'm still very much a vulnerable person, so I'll have to be very careful. I've managed to regain most of the ground I lost a month ago, but in such a different way that I never realized it until 4 or 5 days ago when I started getting letters about my problem.*

*Actually you did more to help me than anyone else – including myself. Thank you my angel, I knew you were God's gift to me, but never realized how all wonderful and powerful you were.*

*The poem and booklet I got today from March 30 was so beautiful and gentle. I felt a touch of God in every page.*

*I'm over the crisis now and will be for the rest of the year here – all because my lover dedicated herself to my happiness. I love you with all my heart and soul.*

*P.S. Shalom, my sweet goddess of love.*

*P.P.S. I'll explain everything, but it will take time to be organized enough mentally to completely explain every aspect. I love you!*

*Your lover,*

*Ben*

**Letter Home 125:** *April 9, 1970; Time – (not noted)*

*Dearest Sue:*

*I love you! I got two more letters and I'm sure you fear my problem is somehow connected with "something you must have done wrong".*

*Please believe me when I tell you all my problems stem from my situation here in Vietnam. As a matter of fact, everything you have done is helping and makes me feel better.*

*All my worrying and crises are caused by loneliness. I miss you so much and I'm so lonely and sad here that my mind cries out. That, in a nut shell is the problem.*

*You keep asking about what you have done to cause this, darling, it is not you, rest assured.*

*Don't worry that your discussions of financial matters is upsetting me. We must discuss money.*

*If you think I'm even considering comparing you and your mother then I deserve to be flogged. I never intend to hurt you, and to compare my wife and lover and angel to your mother is the last thing I care to do.*

*I love you darling, you can trust that, you are the soul reason I am still happy and well and myself here instead of depressed and sick and a brainwashed army Joe.*

*I can't believe it cost $370 round-trip to Hawaii. Does that include a discount because your husband is on R & R? Pan American and United offer such discounts. I'll try and check into it here.*

*Don't worry about the money, I'll send it to you rather than have you take it out of bank. I'll send in May.*

*Cherish is playing – I love you darling. "I could I need you but then you'll realize I want" – and I do, but more than just want, I must have you.*

*My life has matured and developed to a point where I now realize*

*I cannot exist without love, and love cannot exist without you.*

*Sixty-three days to R & R.*

*I look forward so much to being able to live with my wife and child. I'm so proud to read about Johnny and everything you say about him.*

*I know he is going to be someone, but I swore to myself four years ago that I would leave that decision up to him.*

*All I want out of life is happiness and love – you are my prayer answered.*

*I love you Sue, rest in peace, for the sun once again has risen on our harvest life and love.*

*P.S. I'll write you a poem someday.*

*Yours forever,*

*Ben (part-time poet)*

# BLOODY HIGHWAY:
## Driven to Death

### April 12, 1970

**Dangerous Racetrack**

Ben conducted highway patrol for only a couple of weeks before he realized how dangerous MP work was. Not because of firefights, ambushes, or booby traps that the nightly news broadcast but from an unexpected yet too familiar danger—reckless drivers.

It was a man's world on the highway. Driving cargo trucks, Lambretta scooters, and automobiles was exclusively a male role. Although some women rode small mopeds during the day on the streets of Saigon, none ventured onto the highway.

Vietnamese men were generally foolhardy in their efforts to get where they wanted to go. Indifferent to maintaining a safe buffer between vehicles, they drove as if surrounding traffic needed to adjust to them. Drivers occasionally waved a hand signal before changing lanes, but vehicles moved fast, often lurching left and right without warning.

GIs also recklessly drove as if their lives depended on it. Aggression warded off fear about ambushes and expressed hostility toward the Vietnamese. US military convoys careened down highway, encroaching upon any vehicle in its path. They feared the Vietnamese deliberately drove slowly threatening an imminent booby trap.

When it rained—and it poured heavily for long periods—traffic still didn't slow down. Monsoons turned roadways into demolition derbies. Water-covered surfaces coated with a skim of motor oil easily resulted in diminished traction and uncontrollable hydroplaning.

Conducting police operations in such conditions challenged and frustrated MPs since their authority extended to US military vehicles only. In the event of an accident, their primary responsibility was to reach the scene and quickly establish traffic control for safety purposes. They faced physical risks since Vietnamese vehicles constituted seventy percent of the traffic. To protect themselves, some MPs behaved aggressively to intimidate civilians from running traffic control lanes. That reinforced the MPs' reputation of being dangerous when disobeyed while strengthening their influence over civilian behavior.

## Carnage in Bunches

MPs dismissed from guard mount quickly moved to their vehicles. Ben checked his equipment and turned to his new partner Henry Holt. "How do you want to run it today?"

"You drive, I navigate. In case you failed to read the duty roster, we're on Patrol Alpha One today. Go to Ho Nai and then cruise south."

"Roger that. You're the senior MP."

Ben eased out of the company area and turned left to pass in front of LBJ (Long Bien Jail). He turned right onto the base's main road and headed east toward the PMO and the base's main gate.

Radio chatter early in the morning was minimal. Primarily radio checks between mobile patrols and static posts, each reported upon arrival at their assigned positions.

Henry transferred from an infantry unit. In-country for eight months, he ran convoys through Indian Country to fire bases. He was hardened and sarcastic and stood five feet eight inches tall with a thick chest and muscular arms. His fatigues stretched tightly at his biceps.

Ben didn't know him personally, but he heard of his arrogance. He glanced toward him as they turned right onto the highway toward Ho Nai. *This guy's cocky! I hope he isn't one of those who acts before they think. Overconfident men can be stupid and a danger to everyone.*

They patrolled for half an hour in silence. Henry appeared lost in thought, and Ben hesitated to interrupt with casual conversation.

Henry finally broke the silence. "Watch this guy; he's speeding. Pull behind and clock him. He's one of those fucking officers from logistics."

Ben pulled behind and paced the vehicle. *I guess Holt likes to fuck with officers. I'm not getting into an argument with my senior on my first shift.*

He dreaded the friction that arose during a traffic stop. GIs accused MPs of acting Stateside, insisting it was bullshit to pull people over for speeding given the real dangers around them. *Writing speeding tickets is part of our duty, but it feels ridiculous to pull GIs over when everyone's moving at the same speed.*

After a minute of pacing, they confirmed the logistics vehicle was ten miles over the speed limit.

Suddenly, the radio crackled. "Papa Mike Oscar to Alpha One, accident at 316 and 15. Secure the intersection, keep the highway open."

Henry grabbed the mic and responded, "Roger that. Alpha One is ten-one-one to that twenty." He turned to Ben and smirked. "That officer's a lucky bastard. He gets away today. Let's didi to the accident."

Ben swung left to pass the logistics vehicle, relieved to avoid another nasty encounter. Henry flipped on the siren and pointed toward the officer as the vehicle slowed to pull onto the shoulder.

He laughed and crowed, "That ought to make him shit his pants. He knows we had him!"

*Guys like him make GIs hate MPs, but there's nothing I can say.*

They raced south with their siren wailing, pressuring vehicles to move to the right. Ben nudged their jeep tightly against the rear bumper of vehicles that failed to move over as if to ram them. Aggressive driving was one of the MPs' favorite intimidation tactics. Some MPs even fired their weapons in the air when vehicles failed to move out of the way. Bottom-line message: MPs were bad-asses—get the fuck out of their way!

As they approached QL-15, Ben inwardly gasped at the sight of the jumbled mess in the intersection. *A lambretta is mangled under a deuce-and-a-half truck, towering over it like an elephant that's stepped on a water buffalo.*

He swung the jeep alongside the toppled Lambretta and set up to block oncoming traffic. "Oh, shit," he muttered as he stepped from the vehicle. "There're a dozen people in that Lambretta. This is a terrible accident."

"These fucking gooks," Henry snarled. "They don't know how to drive." He lunged from his seat, unsnapped his nightstick, and stepped into the traffic lane. He menacingly swung his nightstick at several Vietnamese vehicles passing too closely to the accident.

Ben continued to investigate. "Looks like they hit one of our trucks."

"Don't be stupid. It's their damn fault for getting in the way. Any idiot would know not to pull that flimsy piece of tin in front of a deuce-and-a-half."

Ben stepped into the traffic lane, pulled his nightstick from its holster, and signaled for traffic to swing wide around them. Positioning their vehicle to shield the accident scene was standard procedure but standing alongside the damaged Lambretta left them dangerously exposed in the road. He watched the heavy traffic and prayed that the flashing emergency lights, along with two MPs standing in the road, would force drivers to slow down.

He glanced again toward the mangled wreckage. He counted a dozen women and children sprawled in a bloody jumble with three wailing as loudly as the jeep's siren. *Damn, we should try to do some first aid for these people.*

Henry noticed Ben's diverted focus and shouted, "Long, pay attention to the traffic! Those gooks aren't our concern. We're not medics!"

That brief exchange distracted his attention from the traffic, and Henry felt a truck brush him. He instinctively swung his nightstick against the vehicle and cursed the driver. "Dinky dau, dou myama!"

Although their responsibility at an accident scene was to prevent secondary collisions, MPs were anxious about the risk of being struck by vehicles trying to squeeze past or careless drivers.

Ben blew three short bursts from his police whistle as a signal to stop.

Agitated by the driver's disregard for police instructions, Henry drew his .45, indicating he'd fire if the driver continued to disobey his commands. MPs typically didn't fire on civilians, but the sight of a drawn pistol added to the tension. Vehicles that wouldn't slow down, particularly if their movement endangered MPs, warranted a warning shot or more.

*Henry's aggressiveness reinforces our reputation as bad-ass police that no one should challenge. We want them to think that way! It serves as self-protection in situations where we really don't have any legal authority. That kind of aggressive behavior can be a powerful weapon that increases compliance and our personal safety.*

## Helpless Observer

Ben spotted a gap in the traffic and turned back toward the accident victims. Two women climbed out of the Lambretta, and another wiggled toward the back of the vehicle. The others didn't move.

*I should do something. Those people are unconscious and need medical attention. It's hard to tell from here, but it isn't right to stand back and do nothing.*

Henry shouted, "Don't move off traffic control! That's your only priority!"

The accident happened one mile from the main gate, but an ambulance didn't come from the base to treat Vietnamese. Jurisdictional rules dictated primary responders to be Vietnamese National Police and local civilian medical services. It was a legal and financial liability for the Army to render medical assistance to the Vietnamese.

Ben stood helplessly at the scene of devastating highway carnage. *What a fucked-up situation. Since the GI driver wasn't injured, and his vehicle was only scratched, our sole duty is to keep traffic moving and secure the scene until the White Mice arrive to take charge.*

Fifteen minutes passed before the White Mice arrived. It was permissible for MPs to stay on-site to provide support but not required.

"Let them have this mess. We're heading to the PMO," Henry directed.

"What about the victims? Some are alive and need medical attention."

"What are you, some kind of do-gooder? These are damn Vietnamese, for God's sake. Why the hell do you care about them? Hell, half of them might be helping Charlie by nightfall. Fuck 'em all!"

"I thought we could help. . ." Ben stammered before being cut off again.

"You help by driving our damn vehicle, Long! You don't understand shit, do you?"

Ben looked back toward the Lambretta. The White Mice directed traffic, seemingly indifferent about the injured. No one checked the victims.

Vietnamese ambulances finally arrived, and Henry waved his hand. "See, I told you the Vietnamese would take care of this."

"Sure took them long enough."

"Their route navigates three miles of narrow streets through Bien Hoa and Tam Hiep before they reach Highway 316. That's a slow drive, even with sirens."

Ben looked again at the sprawl of victims. The image disturbed him, but he fell silent. They climbed into the jeep and drove north toward the main gate.

Henry, less agitated by then, broke the silence. "Long, did you notice the White Mice didn't bother with those people in the Lambretta?"

"Yes. I thought they'd do something."


## Forced Indifference

"Well, that tells you something, doesn't it?" Not waiting for a response, Henry continued, "We have accidents out here every day. You'll learn that it's usually some dumb fuck steering into the path of another vehicle. The Vietnamese drive as if they're the only ones on the highway and expect everyone else to make room for them."

"Okay," Ben mumbled. "I'm not sure what else to say."

"So quit thinking you can make a difference here. These people don't think about life like we do. Maybe it's because there's so many of them. Maybe it's just their stupid Asian mentality. If you try, you'll be the one that's hurt. What makes it worse is my concern that you'll get some of us hurt too."

"Well, several people were badly hurt. I felt we could've provided some medical assistance. It's the decent thing to do."

"I think a few were already dead. Yes, some more may die either from injuries or the piss-poor medical care they'll get at that gook hospital."

"So what are you saying?"

"Shit, man. Do I have to draw you a picture? People here don't even take care of each other. Don't be stupid and think that anything you do will help. Didn't I tell you already? The White Mice didn't even check on their people. If their police don't care, then you're a fool to think you're gonna make a difference."

Ben nodded to the MPs as they approached the main gate. *These guys never leave the base. They have no idea what's happening out there. Maybe they're better off. I wish I didn't know what I just saw and how little we can do.*

He turned and asked, "Okay, what are we doing at the PMO?"

Henry replied with a smile, "You're writing our accident report. It's important you get it down the right way. Describe how the Lambretta swerved in front of the deuce-and-a-half, leaving our GI with no way to avoid the collision."

"We didn't see the accident."

"Long, you graduated from MP School, right? Didn't you learn the basics in accident investigation? You note the position of each vehicle, take statements from drivers, and measure any skid marks as evidence. That GI described the accident, and that's the evidence. The gook pulled right into the path of our military vehicle. Our driver didn't see him swerve before the collision."

"What do I write about the victims?"

Henry's forehead knitted, and he snapped, "Not a fucking thing! Vietnamese aren't part of this report. That's *their* jurisdiction to address. Any deaths or injuries are outside the scope of our report. *They* caused the accident, got it?"

"Roger. Got it," Ben affirmed, and turned toward the workroom.

*Lambretta*

# GLOOM: Death's Shadow

## April 12, 1970

### Contrasting Perspectives

Ben spotted a table filled with friends and weaved his way through the crowded mess hall. "Got room for one more?"

"Sure, we'll let you sit—if you'll buy," Bruce Bugliano quipped.

Greg Pulaski snorted, "Can't imagine who'd pay for this slop."

Ben set his tray down and laughed, "Are you kidding? This is probably the best food on the base. You can't beat mystery meat stirred into leftovers. And look at these dimpled peas; I'll bet they're fresh-picked from the garden."

"Glad to hear you still got your sense of humor. Heard you had a bad one today," Greg stated.

"Every day there seems to be something crazy," Bruce added. "Can't complain about being bored doing the same old shit."

"As opposed to the boredom of our food choices," Tucker Bronson chimed in.

"Seriously, though, what happened?" Greg asked.

Ben mumbled with a mouthful of food, "It was ugly. A Lambretta packed with civilians got flipped and crushed by a deuce-and-a-half. Bodies scattered everywhere, with kids mixed into the mess."

"Was our guy okay?" Tucker interrupted.

"Nice attitude, asshole!" Greg barked. "Worry about the guy in the big truck."

Tucker pointed his fork at Greg and responded, "We see these accidents every day. There's nothing we can do about crazy gook drivers. Their mess is their business to deal with. We're only responsible for taking care of our own ."

Bruce shook his head. "That's cold, man."

"It is what it is," Tucker countered. "Don't you realize that getting emotionally involved will drive you crazy?"

"Well, thanks for that sage advice. Back to the human side of the conversation," Greg continued. "Ben, tell us what happened."

"There were probably several dead, but I don't know about the others. We left after the White Mice and ambulances arrived."

"That's the way it happens, isn't it?" Greg said. "We kill 'em and maim 'em and then leave a mess for somebody else to clean up."

"Wow, you're in a sour mood!" Tucker exclaimed. "Were these people friends of yours? As I said, don't get emotionally involved. It ain't worth it, and it doesn't matter."

Ben sighed, "The hard part is we're required to stand back and observe. There's so much misery, and people are screaming. I feel we should help, but—"

"You know damn well we aren't allowed to touch them," Tucker interrupted. "That's how the brass protects themselves—and us."

"It's a tough situation, but orders are orders," Bruce added.

"Doesn't mean we have to like it," Greg argued. "It's not right. We should help where we can."

"When the Army brings that up for a vote, then you'll have a chance to change the policy," Tucker replied cynically.

It'll snow here before that day comes," Greg asserted.

"That's my point. Officers make the decisions, soldiers obey. Quit your bitching! When the Army wants you to have an opinion, they'll issue one to you," Tucker sarcastically replied.

Bruce stood as if to leave. "I'm done here."

"It's been interesting," Ben replied. "Thanks for the unsolicited advice, as if I asked for it."

"Fuck you too!" Tucker snapped, and left the table.

"Don't pay any attention to him," Greg suggested. "I think these accidents have gotten to Tucker, and he deals with the stress by being angry and pushing everyone away."

## Both Sides Now

Bruce turned toward Ben as they left the mess hall. "He's an ass, don't pay attention to him. Let's get a beer. Bet you could use one."

Ben nodded, and they headed to the EM Club.

"Maybe it's noisier in here, but I think we'll find it's more peaceful," Bruce said as they stepped inside the air-conditioned club.

"Yeah, that got pretty intense. Those guys have strong opinions."

"No lack of that around here," Bruce declared. "Let me buy the first round."

"You're right, I could use one or six."

Bruce returned with four beers. "I thought four would be a good start. If I'd bought six, we'd have a warm one when we opened number three. Besides, you should pay. Next round's on you."

"Great plan. I like the way you think."

They guzzled their first cans, listening to the jukebox blaring a popular song by the Animals, "We Gotta Get Outta this Place."

*Bruce's right; even with the loud music, it's more peaceful in here without all that arguing.*

They pulled the tabs on their second cans. "I was in a bad accident a couple of years ago," Ben confided.

"Oh, yeah?" Bruce took a long swig and studied Ben's face.

"It was Memorial Day in my senior year of high school."

"High school, huh? That was a while ago, right?"

"It'll be four years in May."

"Four years – that's a lifetime ago."

Ben stared toward the jukebox with a blank expression. "Today brought it all back."

"Okay . . ."

"We were idiots on our way to a drinking party."

Bruce nodded, took another sip, and continued to listen.

"We didn't get there. A drunk driver broadsided us. Our car was totaled."

"Sounds like it was bad."

"We rolled three times; I was thrown out on impact and landed a hundred feet away, three feet from a utility pole. Coulda been killed."

"Did you get pretty messed up?"

"I was knocked unconscious. I had extensive injuries, punctured right shoulder, bloody smashed face, and skin shredded off the back of my hands. I was in the hospital two weeks and on crutches for two more."

"The back of your hands?"

"My leather high school jacket protected my arms from abrasions."

"You must have looked awful."

"I guess. I regained consciousness in the emergency room and heard my mom shrieking about how bad I looked."

"Lucky guy."

"There but for the grace of God . . ."

Bruce fell silent.

"Today's accident brought that memory back. I'm thinking about accidents from both sides now."

"Sounds like that line in the Joni Mitchell song about clouds."

"Seeing those people lying on the pavement in their blood made me wonder how horrible I must've looked, crumpled and bleeding next to a utility pole. It's intense enough to be the first one at the scene of an accident, but it feels awful to stand back and do nothing while people scream and bleed out."

"Sounds like intense emotions got triggered."

"Brings a deeper understanding for both sides of a situation." He stood and said, "Time for a break; I'm gonna pee and get more beer."

"Good idea. I think we're ready for another."

## Numb Detachment

Ben returned with four more cans, and Bruce pulled a tab and took a long swallow. "You know, we'll see plenty more accidents. That highway's dangerous."

Ben took a sip of his beer. "I know, and I wonder how I'll deal with it."

"You don't have a choice; you'll follow orders. Don't risk an Article 15. It's not worth it."

"Maybe you're right, but it seems wrong to be a bystander. Given what I know about both sides of an accident, how can I reconcile doing nothing when I understand the importance of quick action to save lives?"

"We face plenty of contradictory situations over here; the only way I know is to disconnect. You have to forget who you are. Then you need to put on a disguise and pretend to be someone else. It's how you'll survive emotionally and mentally. Otherwise, these conflicts are going to tear you apart."

Ben's head dropped. "I feel like that's telling me to betray myself and become indifferent to someone else's pain."

"It's not me who's suggesting it but it's what our orders dictate."

"But that's not who I am! This contrast is too extreme," Ben protested.

"You're in the Army now, as the old song says."

"I hate this. Am I supposed to act like I don't care? How can I live with such a dichotomy?"

"You'll do what all of us have had to do—bow before *the Man*, act like you appreciate his generosity, and keep your opinions to yourself. Otherwise, you'll find yourself tied to the whipping post. That's not the path you want to take."

Ben shook his head in disgust. "I'll need an emotional lobotomy to go along with those orders."

"Better a lobotomy than an execution."

Ben stared at his can and chugged the last of that beer. "How does a guy sever his emotional jugular vein?"

"I think you have the answer in your hand," Bruce quipped as he drained his can. "Alcohol numbs the senses, brother."

"Numb my brain, dull my senses? What a simple solution."

"It's worked for centuries. That's why so many get drunk."

Ben stared toward the television. "So all I need to do is detach and become numb. Then my conflicts go away?"

## Shattered Lives

"It's that simple."

"And terrible," Ben added.

"Nobody said life was nice, or even fair. We're in a messy place, and we do what we have to do to get through it. If it means killing people, we kill people. If it means killing a part of ourselves, then we kill a part of ourselves."

Ben pulled the tab on the final can and took a long swallow. "It's a version of committing suicide—I kill my ethical and emotional self."

Bruce nodded, opened his last can, and gulped his beer. "Here in Vietnam, everything we value eventually dies – one way or another."

Ben stared silently at his beer can.

Bruce continued, "Think about those accident victims—some died, and that shattered their families' lives. Some victims recovered, but they may be disabled or scarred. Their lives are shattered and changed too."

Lost in thought, Ben recalled another painful memory. "I've seen many damaged children. Some were street urchins and thieves, others had traumatized bodies in a hospital in Cholon. They're likely haunted with anxiety and fear about the next danger lurking in the shadows."

"This place shatters lives. We shouldn't expect that we'll be immune."

"But if I shield myself by detached numbing, I'll be shattering my own life."

"When the outcome's inevitable, I suppose the method's irrelevant," Bruce concluded as he finished his last beer.

Ben finished his last beer too. *I suppose that's right when I don't have any control over the outcome of any of these poor people's circumstances. It's not up to me whether they live or die, but it is up to our Creator. Please help us, God....*

# TAN AN: Major Delivery

## April 14, 1970

### Special Assignment

"Things never get boring here, do they?" Ben asked Greg Pulaski, standing at the duty roster board.

"What do you mean?"

"Today, they've put me on a special assignment. I have no idea what that means. I hope I'm not on a bullshit work detail."

"Whatever it is, you'll need to wait until guard mount. You know the Army doesn't let you know until the last minute."

"Yeah. Sure wouldn't want anyone to know in advance what's happening. That's not the Army way," Ben snarled sarcastically.

"They don't want guys to overthink. Come on; we're gonna be late."

All stood at attention and listened as the Platoon Sergeant read through the sequence of duty assignments – first static posts, then mobile patrols, and finally, special assignments.

"Rogers and Long, you're on special assignment," Sergeant Simon announced.

Ben rolled his eyes. *No shit, Dick Tracy. I already know I'm on a special assignment. I read it on the duty roster. What I want to know are the details.*

The Sergeant dismissed the platoon, and everyone moved to their vehicles.

He waved his clipboard toward Danny Rogers. "You're going to draw a vehicle, drive to Newport PMO, and pick up a passenger for delivery to Tan An."

"Prisoner, Sergeant?"

"No, you're transporting an officer from Battalion who you'll deliver to the 188th MP Company. You've done convoy duty on QL-4, so you drive. We know you can find Tan An and not get lost in Saigon."

Danny nodded, "After six months in-country, I know my way around."

"Long, draw a weapon," the Sergeant continued. "You're riding shotgun as Rogers's backup on the return trip."

"Sounds like fun," Danny exclaimed, grinning widely. "I love road trips."

"Smart-ass! Don't get delayed in Saigon on the way back."

"Sergeant, I'd never do that," he declared, feigning innocence.

"You know what I mean!" the Sergeant snarled.

"Clear as a bell in hell, Sergeant."

"Get the fuck out of here. I don't have time for your shit!"

Danny turned toward Ben, "This'll be a long, hot drive. Go to the motor pool and get a vehicle with a top. I'll go to HQ and sign us out."

Ben returned to the company area with a covered jeep, and they were ready to roll in thirty minutes. They drove through the main gate and began the fifteen-mile journey to Saigon.

At Newport Bridge, Danny accelerated to climb the steep span. He needed to break firmly on the descent to safely turn at the bottom and curve back beneath the bridge. Traveling another quarter-mile, he stopped at Newport's entrance and explained their assignment to the MP operating the gate.

Donnie Westfield was gate MP, Ben's friend from Fort Gordon MP School. They briefly exchanged updates about duty assignments and laughed as they recounted their Saigon Tea incident. (See 1st Moon: Innocence, Story 6 ~ Streetwalking Blues).

Danny interrupted the friendly banter, "We need to get to the PMO."

Donnie pointed toward a white trailer with a wooden ramp that resembled a construction site office. "You can see it from here. Ben, great to see you again."

"You too. Stay safe."

Ben trudged up the all too familiar ramp, where he frequently visited that PMO during his 300th duty. He stepped inside and spotted Staff Sergeant Mac Waverly. *What a small world! Mac was desk sergeant when I was on that Vietnamese prisoner delivery assignment to a hospital in Cholon. He notified me about the Red Cross message announcing Johnny's birth.*

"Kilo!" Mac exclaimed as his face lit with excitement. He stood and reached over the high desk, extending his right hand to greet him.

"Mac," Ben replied. "Great to see you. It's like an old home week."

Recognizing Danny as ranking MP, Mac addressed him facetiously. "So what brings you here today? Are you delivering this guy as a prisoner?"

Danny recognized the camaraderie. "Ben must be guilty of something, but today we're here to escort an officer to Tan An."

Mac resumed his desk sergeant persona. "Yes, we heard a patrol would arrive to pick up Major Johnson. He needs a ride to the 188th. We'll let him know you're here."

He sent the clerk to fetch the officer and redirected his attention to Ben. "How's that bouncing baby boy doing?"

"Johnny's almost three months old. I've been getting pictures. I hope to take R & R in Hawaii in June."

"That's great! And how's mama?"

"She's living with her parents. She's good, but her mom can be overprotective."

"That's better for mama than caring for a baby alone. At least she's got help."

The clerk returned with Major Johnson, a tall black officer in his early 30s. He swung a duffel bag into Ben's chest. "This goes with the Major. See that it's secured."

Ben and Mac exchanged nods, acknowledging that socializing ended. There'd be no more small talk now that an officer was present.

"Sir, we'll provide a safe escort through Saigon to Tan An," Danny explained as they walked to the jeep. Ben secured the duffel bag in the back of the jeep.

## Hat in the Delta

Danny functioned as principal contact with Major Johnson. They briefly discussed the travel itinerary before all climbed into the jeep and exited the compound. The Major rode in silence with Ben behind him. *I don't think there's going to be much chit chat. It's going to be a long ride. I feel like baggage back here, but at least I'm in the back and won't have to deal with him.*

Ninety percent of the vehicles traveling into Saigon from the north crossed the Newport Bridge. The Americans built Highway 316 as a more secure route for US military traffic from Long Binh Army Base and Bien Hoa Air Base. Although QL-1 was Vietnam's National Highway, it was a two-lane road that crossed the Saigon River five miles upstream at Gia Dinh, making it a slower and riskier route into Saigon.

They drove out of Newport into a traffic circle, merging into the traffic into Saigon. Ben soon realized his baggage status had benefits.

*I'm invisible in the back so that I can take in all the sights.*

He immediately noticed familiar smells and choked on the truck exhaust as they crept along the four-lane road. The pungent odor of nuoc mam stung his nostrils. *Shit! I hoped I'd never smell that disgusting stuff again.*

He also noticed the Vietnamese paid little attention to passing traffic. *Being in a vehicle is safer than walking. I wouldn't feel comfortable here. I'd draw too much attention and would have to be on guard against boy-sans and check every alley. I'm lucky to be in the back! I can check out all the scenery since we're creeping at walking speed.*

Multi-story plaster-walled buildings with businesses and residences passed. Mobile-cart vendors occupied most spaces along the road, and makeshift shacks with corrugated roofs filled other areas. Those structures shared one bizarre characteristic – their walls consisted of four-by-eight aluminum sheets embossed with Coca-Cola labels, indicating they were panels to be cut and rolled into beverage cans.

Images of street-cart vendors selling fruit and noodles, boy-sans running alongside vehicles begging for money, and men squatting in small groups captivated Ben. The sights created a hypnotic effect as they passed a blur of pharmacies, restaurants, electronic stores, and street carts.

Narrow alleys intermittently punctuated the continuous row of buildings. Ben glanced into each alley and recalled the path to Mama-san's parlor. He watched women appear and disappear; and imagined how the alleys deeply weaved throughout the city. (See 2nd Moon: Temptation, Story 22 ~ Mama San's Parlor, and Story 27 ~ Mind Rip).

*I can't fathom the complexity of the network of alleys. I remember there weren't any vendors in the alleys, and women shopped on the main road for bread, fish, and vegetables.*

Ten minutes into Ben's daydream, they arrived at another

roundabout. *This place is insane! How does this sea of humanity manage to navigate these circles? It's like we're swirling in a drain, with vehicles circling instead of disappearing down a central drain.*

Danny cursed the Vietnamese drivers who pushed in front of his vehicle as he navigated toward the second exit.

Ben caught his breath. *Whew! A guy could get dizzy in these traffic circles.*

They angled to the west along a road that connected Newport and Pershing Field. Moving on Cong Ly, they soon reached Third Field Hospital and Tan Son Nhut Air Base. Traffic thinned, and Danny accelerated to forty miles an hour. In another mile, they turned right at the racetrack and accelerated to fifty on Highway QL-4. Saigon's dense, smog-filled streets shrunk behind them and lush green rice paddies now bordered the roadway. *We must be at the start of the Delta!*

Ben glanced back toward Saigon, and a gust of wind pushed the bill of his hat. He felt it lift but couldn't prevent it from flying off. Stunned, he barely caught a glimpse of the hat as it sailed into a rice paddy. *Oh shit! We're moving so fast I lost my hat before I could react! I feel stupid and don't want to ask that we stop.*

He felt torn over his dilemma and couldn't relax. *This scenic ride has turned into dread about how to deal with my lost hat. I shouldn't say anything. The Sergeant will chew me out for not having enough sense to hold onto my hat. Then he'll light into me about causing a delay to go back for my hat. Anyway, stopping in the middle of nowhere isn't safe. We probably won't even find the damn hat. What can I do? The hat's far behind us. Any mention of it will only make everyone mad. What are we supposed to do? Turn around and search several miles for a stupid hat?*

He tried to recapture the enjoyment of the ride but became consumed with worry. *My anxiety about that damn hat has blotted out the beauty of these green rice paddies and palm trees. Frankly, who gives a shit about it anyway? It's not like I lost my M-16 or the duffel bag!*

No one noticed Ben's dilemma as they silently rolled along QL-4. Gradually worry receded as he hoped no one would see his hat was missing.

## Tan An

The endless stream of paddies presented a bland contrast to Saigon's diversely colored buildings as they continued to travel through the Delta. Grassy thatched huts seemed mundane compared to the city's multi-storied structures.

"We're here," Danny announced. Tan An looked like another cluster of grass thatch huts along the highway.

"Where?" Major Johnson asked. Being new in-country, he didn't know what to expect. He'd seen Long Binh and Saigon, but he didn't anticipate ending up at a remote base among rice paddies and thatched huts.

"Tan An is a small village, sir," Danny explained. "Its only significance is it straddles QL-4, and we have a base nearby to help secure the highway between Saigon and My To. Cookies provide our security."

"Cookies? What does that mean?"

"They're 9th Infantry grunts. They conduct patrols on the dikes to check for Charlie setting up ambushes against convoys."

Within two minutes, they passed through the small village of Tan An into another open paddy area. They arrived at the base gate, and the MP on duty waved them through. Danny pulled around and parked. With hardly a glance, Major Johnson ordered Ben to bring his bag.

He lifted the Major's duffel bag and stood ready to follow the next instruction. The Major noticed Ben wasn't wearing a hat. "Where's your hat, soldier?"

"It blew out in the Delta, sir."

"What? Why didn't you say anything?"

Ben stammered to find a rationale for his inaction. "I didn't want to make a scene, sir. Besides, it would have made us late."

"You should have spoken up. How are we going to get it now?"

Before Ben could reply, the Major added, "You can't be without a hat. It's a uniform violation."

Ben stared at the officer, not sure what to say. *We can't go back and search for that hat. It's not worth the time or risk. Besides, who really cares? And uniform violation? Give me a break! Who gives a shit out here if you have a hat?*

Major Johnson continued, "I can write you up for this, soldier. You're an MP; you know better. You should be a role model, not a bad example."

Lost for words, Ben glanced at Danny, who recognized Ben's dilemma. "Major, you're right. Long *is* stupid and in violation of uniform policy. But we're not going to find that hat. I'll be sure he gets a reprimand if that's your intention. For now, we'll go to Supply and get him another hat so that he's properly attired."

"You're a good MP, Rogers. See that this soldier gets his act together." With the crisis in military order resolved, the Major headed toward HQ.

Danny turned to Ben and directed, "Get his bag delivered and get a fucking hat from Supply. We don't need this bullshit. Then meet me in the mess hall. We're going to get some chow before we start back to Long Binh."

Ben ran the errands and reached the mess hall with a replacement hat. He sat across from Danny, who shoveled down a plate of mashed potatoes and pork chops.

"Okay, Ben," he explained between bites. "We're going to make something worthwhile out of this day. I saved your ass with the Major

– you owe me. We should take a detour in Saigon, but I need you to keep something under your hat. Get me?"

Ben smiled sheepishly at the play on words. "Yes, now that I have a hat."

Danny laughed and continued, "Right! This fucking hat thing is just so much bullshit. But seriously, I need to make sure our detour is just between you and me. Nobody needs to be the wiser for it. You understand my point?"

"Clear as a bell in hell!" Ben confirmed, repeating the phrase from the morning.

"Great. Let's pitch this crap and go get something better."

## Tu Do Street

They rolled out the gate onto QL-4. Ben felt relieved to leave Tan An and the STRAC Major in the rearview mirror. He firmly pulled down his hat and stared as they sped past familiar thatched dwellings. *The ride back to Saigon feels faster than the trip down. I'm excited about where we're going, now that I don't have that hat stress hanging over my head.*

"By the way, why did the desk sergeant call you Kilo?" Danny asked.

"He gave me that nickname after I shared a college story with him."

"College story, huh? Was that related to math or something more interesting?"

Ben smiled and nodded. "There was plenty of math involved, but it was an extracurricular project. It had to do with weights and measures."

Danny laughed and replied, "Okay, I'm getting the drift. If it's what I'm thinking, you and I'll get along just fine."

"I'll just say that a kilo weighs two point two pounds. That's important to know when you're dealing with bulk goods and have to get your portions right."

"Enough said, I'm digging you," Danny quipped as he raised his thumb and index finger to his lips and drew a long breath.

Ben examined the roadside as they neared Saigon's outskirts, where he thought his hat blew off. It seemed unlikely he'd find it, but he felt compelled to try.

Danny noticed and barked, "Don't think we're going to stop for that damn hat! It's cost us enough already. Besides, you got a new one."

They passed the racetrack, turned toward Tan Son Nhut, passed Third Field Hospital, and turned onto Cong Ly Boulevard. Ben smiled as they passed Mama-san's alley and crossed the canal into downtown. When they reached the Presidential Palace, he peered through the gates. *This area is all familiar because I've been in-country for a long time. I know my way around and won't get lost.*

Danny slowly cruised past the USO and pulled to the curb on Tu Do Street. They barely stopped when a 716th MP jeep pulled alongside. "What are you soldiers doing here? Show me your passes."

The ongoing problems with drugs, prostitution, and black-market activities in Saigon required all GIs to carry passes. MPs heavily patrolled the Tu Do bar strip to control criminal activity.

Danny subtly pivoted to display his 18th MP Brigade patch. "Yes, sir. We just escorted an MP Officer to Tan An, who's new in-country. We were assigned to be sure he had secure transport."

The 716th MP recognized the 18th Brigade patch. "You're an MP? I don't recognize you."

"Yes, we're out of Long Binh. We patrol the highway from Long Binh to Newport. We stopped for a few minutes to break up our trip back."

The other 716th MP stepped up. "Okay, we didn't see your patch. Everything's good here."

Ben appreciated the police code that cops always covered for other cops. No matter what unit, MPs didn't hassle other MPs. That was a lifesaver because neither he nor Danny carried a pass.

The MP jeep pulled away, and two bar girls stepped out onto the sidewalk and grabbed Rogers's arm. "You back. Long time no see, MP. Buy me Saigon Tea?"

As the girls pulled Danny into the bar, he turned toward Ben. "I'm a regular here. Let's get inside before anybody else sees us."

They stepped into the darkened bar, and more money-hungry bar girls smothered them with affection. "You buy me Saigon Tea," one wetly whispered into Ben's ear.

"MP numba one," cooed another.

"We love MPs," a third one declared as she pressed her body against Danny's shoulder.

He had two girls clinging to him. "We have sixty minutes, so don't waste time getting warmed up."

They pulled MPC (military paper certificates) from their pockets and slapped the bills onto the table. One of the bar girls grabbed the money and hurried away.

Ben shouted to Danny over the giggling, "So, what do you think the Major would say about this? Since he was so uptight about a lost hat, I can only imagine how intense his reaction would be to *this* behavior!"

"Don't mean nothing, he's not here," Danny mumbled from behind a pair of pawing bar girls.

*Flooded paddies*

*USO area*

## Letter Home 126: *April 16, 1970 Time – (Not noted)*

*My Darling Sue:*

*I love you. Time is flying here and I can hardly believe the date. I hope you are not upset because I have not written much. I really don't have any time. I'm starting to get organized here and may be able to write more in a week or two.*

*I've been driving every day on that highway from Saigon to Long Binh. It is the most dangerous road I have ever seen and when it rains (pours is a better word) these stupid gooks speed up instead of slow down.*

*We had an accident out there a couple of days ago and nine people died. It is normal for monsoon season, which starts in May or June.*

*I've been run off the road several times already because to ARVN's (Vietnamese soldiers) hate MPs. This job takes 110 percent of my energy and concentration because even "routine patrol" is dangerous.*

*Two weeks ago I had a truck turn a corner in front of me and drop six (140 lbs.) artillery shells in my path. I almost blew my mind – each of these shells has a kill ratio of 300 meters.*

*I had a day off two days ago but they sent me to Tan An to escort a Major. Tan An is 30 miles south of Saigon into the Delta.*

*They have made me the patrol supervisor's driver because I'm a "sharp looking MP." I must confess I hate the whole place here and the job is very trying.*

*I am faking everything here and feel like an actor. The only thing that keeps me from giving up is your love, which is strong enough and worthwhile enough to do anything for.*

*I am so skinny now I'd pass for the 98-lb. weakling. It is so hot that I am irritable all the time and edgy – that probably is my major problem. If you can send any snow or cold weather.*

*I'm fitting in here very well with the guys – but of course no one can even guess that there is more to me than the front they see. It is just as well. I'd probably go to jail for thinking – it is illegal you know.*

*I've got many pictures of Johnny, but please send me one of you. I love you, Sue, and don't expect to make me happy by talking about Johnny all the time – his time will come, but I need you.*

*All my love, forever, Ben*

# SUPERVISOR'S DRIVER:
# New Lens

## April 17, 1970

### Random Assignment

"What the hell does 'Driver' mean?" Ben blurted out, staring at the duty roster.

No one replied.

"What the fuck, aren't most of us drivers on patrol?"

A voice behind him piped up, "That means you're the Patrol Supervisor's driver, dumb ass."

Ben continued his rant, "What's that mean?"

"It means you're assigned to drive Sergeant Simon all day. He's the Patrol Supervisor; you're his driver."

"Why am I the driver? How did this get figured out?"

"You're an idiot, Long. It's random, and it's the luck of the draw—unless there's a reason he wants you."

Ben turned to read the name on the MP's fatigue—Succors. He didn't know him.

Another voice added, "Well, maybe Long's a suck-up. Or maybe

Long's one of Sergeant Simon's snitches, and he's been watching the rest of us!"

"Bullshit!" Ben snapped as he turned to see Tucker Bronson.

"Yeah, that's just what a stool pigeon would say," Tucker declared, implying Ben might be a spy for Sergeant Simon. "We know Simon's a hard-ass and will do anything to keep us in line. Maybe he picked you for a driver because you're his guy and will report on us."

Ben grew more annoyed. "That's a load of crap. I don't know him any more than the rest of you."

Sergeant Simon walked up, and everyone froze. He knifed his way through the group, stood in front of the duty roster, and barked, "Okay, reading class is over. Move out to guard mount so we can get this show on the road." He turned to Ben and directed, "Long, meet me at HQ after roll call to go over your assignment."

Ben felt suspicious glares from some guys as they moved toward the assembly area. *Simon's style must be to control his platoon by creating dissent among us.*

No one spoke as they assembled for guard mount. Tension in the platoon was already high because most guys weren't sure how to deal with Sergeant Simon. All they knew was what they heard at the meeting—he was a hard-ass, and men would toe the line or else!

## A New Lens

The Sergeant reviewed assignments and dismissed the men to move to their patrol vehicles. Drivers rechecked their equipment and departed the company area toward the main gate. Ben followed Sergeant Simon to HQ. *I've not been a supervisor's driver before. I don't know what this duty entails.*

The Sergeant walked past the company clerk and disappeared into a back area containing offices for officers. The clerk motioned for Ben to sit near his desk. "You'll wait here until the Patrol Supervisor finishes his meeting with the Captain. When he comes out, you'll drive him to the PMO."

Ben glanced around the office. It was the second time he'd been inside HQ, but its layout was the same as the 300's HQ. Every desk contained neat stacks of material, and bulletin boards were clearly labeled. *The Army organizes everything down to the last detail.*

Ben didn't see Sergeant Simon come out of the Captain's office.

"Long, daydreaming about being a clerk, or are you going to get a move on?" he snapped as he headed toward the door.

Startled by the Sergeant's voice, Ben leaped to his feet, knowing he needed to make a positive first impression. *Oh, shit, better not start on the wrong foot!*

"Go to the PMO," Sergeant Simon directed as they climbed in the jeep.

Ben exited the company area and drove slowly down the two-hundred-yard descent toward LBJ's front gate. *I'd better not fuck up, or I might end up in there.*

The PMO was only a mile beyond LBJ, just inside the main gate, but Ben was so nervous the trip felt like three miles. Finally, the Sergeant snapped, "If you drive any slower, it'll be lunch before we get on the highway. Get a move on!"

The PMO building was a one-story structure and twice the length of a barracks. Provost Marshal was painted in large letters on the front with the Military Police's crossed pistols emblem in yellow and green.

They parked and entered the air-conditioned building. The receiving desk was just inside the entrance, massive and tall like a judge's bench. Visitors felt small when they stood before that imposing structure. *Psychological intimidation is a powerful weapon in the police toolbox. That desk sure makes the message loud and clear that it's the dominant force in this setting.*

Sergeant Simon presented himself by name, rank, and purpose. The desk sergeant acknowledged him and authorized them to proceed to a workroom where several MPs sat around a table. Ben followed him and took a seat in the corner. He listened to the radio chatter between patrols and the PMO before realizing he sat in the communications center. *This spot gives a vantage point to the entire Military Police operations.*

The PMO was crowded, with many MPs in the building, but attention to radio communications appeared casual. Most didn't pay attention because they were engaged in other duties. Some wrote reports while others processed prisoners. A small group of MPs huddled in conversation, but their voices drowned out the radio traffic.

After ninety minutes, Ben gained a valuable insight into operational communications. The radio operator appeared to be the only MP solely focused on radio traffic. *This insight is intriguing! Now that I've seen the process from the inside, I see some useful aspects of the system. I can change how I communicate when on patrol.*

Sergeant Simon finished his business. "Long, let's move. We need to do our morning check. I want to confirm that everything's going well out there."

## By the Book

When they reached their vehicle, the Sergeant radioed the PMO. "Papa Sierra Alpha back in service."

*That would be a critical message to hear if I was relaxing on a static post.*

They exited the main gate and turned north toward the 90th Replacement Compound. "Swing along the entrance road and come up behind their position. I don't want the men to see us coming."

Ben nodded and steered to the right, hugging the base perimeter near the west gate. He swung sharply left and approached SP-18's position from behind. The MPs relaxed in their vehicle, faced toward the highway, and didn't see the approaching jeep. He eased alongside

SP18's left, positioning Sergeant Simon three feet from the static post vehicle. The Sergeant's sudden appearance startled the unwary MPs.

"Men, how's your morning going?" he asked matter of factly.

"Good, sir," replied the MP in the driver's seat as he hurried to put on his helmet and straighten his uniform.

"I'm checking that we're staying sharp out here," the Sergeant clarified.

Both MPs nodded at Simon and then glared at Ben.

"Is there anything you need?" the Sergeant asked.

"Everything is good. Thanks," replied the senior MP.

"Good. Things look good here. Be sure to stay sharp and keep your uniform squared away. Remember that helmets stay on at all times. Carry on." Sergeant Simon turned to Ben and directed, "Let's continue our patrol. Head south." They pulled onto the highway and turned south.

Ben worried about how the MPs reacted. *Those guys were caught off guard. I hope they don't blame me for that inspection ambush.*

"Patrol Supervisors need to inspect each post once per shift, twice if possible," the Sergeant explained. "I like to catch them in the act. Inspections allow me to evaluate alertness and protocol. They need to stay sharp out there. Uniforms, including helmets, must be proper at all times. Appearance is an important indicator of military discipline."

Their arrival at the next static post didn't offer the same element of surprise since they were visible for several hundred yards while crossing the Dong Nai River Bridge. The MPs were ready when they pulled up to SP-16's position. Sergeant Simon repeated his canned greeting, pleased to find the static post MPs looking sharp and alert. He pointed toward the highway, signaling Ben to continue south toward SP-14. Both remaining static posts appeared to be alert and ready for inspection when Sergeant Simon and Ben arrived at their locations.

The Sergeant complimented the MPs, "You men look sharp. Glad to see you're demonstrating proper military discipline and esprit de corps."

Ben noticed the difference in the MPs' reactions. *We didn't surprise these last posts. I wonder if someone tipped them off that we were coming?*

Sergeant Simon finished the SP-11 inspection. "It's eleven a.m., and we're down here near Newport. We'd better start back to the base so I can submit my report before we go to chow."

"Roger that," Ben confirmed. *The Patrol Supervisor's duty looks more like a show than real action.*

As they traveled north and passed SP-14 and SP-16, each post waved at the Patrol Supervisor's vehicle. The Sergeant returned their wave and smiled.

*Are they flipping us off, showing they're aware of our game?*

They arrived at the PMO, and the desk sergeant waved them through to the workroom.

*I have some time; I'll wander around and check this place out. I'd like a better understanding of what's happening.* Ben stepped into the radio operator room and asked, "What would flag attention from the patrols?"

"Routine check-in is normal," the operator explained. "However, anything unusual gets flagged and is forwarded to the Patrol Supervisor."

"What's unusual?" Ben innocently asked.

"We expect patrols to regularly let us know where they are and what they're doing. When we don't hear from them, or when they report a problem, that's a flag, and I contact the supervisor."

Ben nodded.

"When the supervisor gets notified, he decides whether he needs to go on the highway to check on patrols."

Ben paused and clarified, "So regular check-in is expected?"

The radio operator frowned. "Of course. You should know the

protocol. Irregularities and lapses trigger the supervisor to come out looking for you."

Ben leaned back and replied, "Well, nobody wants that unless a situation needs his presence."

"Right. Patrol MPs need to have their act together and know what to do. If the supervisor has to come out to check on you, then you're probably already fucking up and in deep shit."

"Yeah, nobody wants to have the supervisor come down on them because they fucked up," Ben agreed and walked back to the workroom.

## Leader Presence

Sergeant Simon finished his morning report and instructed Ben to drive to the company for chow. As they entered the mess hall, Ben reflected on his opportunity. *I want the Sergeant to have a positive impression of me. I'll ask about how I can become a Sergeant someday.*

They sat at a corner table. "Sarge, can I ask a couple of things?" Ben asked.

"Sure, shoot."

"I earned E-4 in February, and I expect a promotion to E-5 might be possible if I do the right things. But I'm not sure what indicates a guy is qualified for hard stripes."

"What are you asking? Talk straight."

"Okay. Being a Sergeant means being a leader. What's your advice on how to lead men? Listening to you and Sergeant Rockwell the other day, I heard a big difference in leadership styles. Why?"

Simon snorted, "Hell, I can't explain Sergeant Rockwell's style. What I know comes from my background and time in the field. I'm not schooled like you college boys, but it's fucking clear to me that life's a better teacher than books and classrooms."

"Okay, so how did you get to where you are?"

"My education came from the school of hard knocks. I worked in construction, and my dad was the foreman. I learned right away that some guys show up ready to work with the right tools, but there are a few who aren't so good. Sometimes it's so bad that you're lucky if they show up at all."

Ben nodded, listening intently.

The Sergeant continued, "When I arrived in-country, I found that the lessons I learned on the construction site applied here too. People are people, and you need to figure out who's bringing what. Then you know what you need to do to lead them."

He paused, looked carefully into Ben's eyes, and added, "You can have confidence in some guys to always show up on time and dress for the dance. But others are fuck-ups and don't care about meeting expectations. Mission success depends on the quality and commitment of men."

Ben stared at his plate as he chewed a gristly piece of cubed steak.

"The key responsibility for a leader is to identify who's reliable, who's a slacker, and take action to make sure everyone's ready to do their job."

Ben didn't look up, and Simon challenged, "Long, are you present? I need to know I'm not wasting my breath on you."

Ben stammered at his aggressiveness, "Yes, I'm listening."

"Bullshit! Being present means you're actively engaged. I don't see that behavior from you."

"I'm sorry. I'm listening."

The Sergeant grew more irritated and pressed, "Damn it! Don't be sorry, that's a weakness. A leader must always be ready and take action, even when there's no opening. If you want to be a leader, you have to be ahead of all the others. You have to understand what I'm saying, what I'm not saying, and what I should be saying. Then you jump into action and take charge of the situation."

Ben floundered and replied, "I heard you say some men are ready and some not ready, some committed and some not too committed. I get that. But what are the actions that a leader takes to manage those people?"

The Sergeant leaned back and flashed half a smile. "That's good, Long. There might be some hope for you after all."

Ben leaned forward, relieved his response wasn't as stupid as he felt.

"But before I lay it out, I have a question for you. I read your file and saw you were a squad leader in AIT and attended the two-week Leadership Training Detachment in Fort Gordon. What did you learn from those experiences?"

Ben laid down his fork and took a deep breath. *Oh, shit—test time. What am I going to say that will make a good impression? I've got thirty seconds to come up with a smart answer.*

"Go ahead, think first. That's a good sign."

"Well, the first thing that comes to mind is that everyone must have the same understanding of expectations."

"Okay . . ."

"The second thing is I remember a guy in my squad who didn't care about keeping his footlocker in proper order for inspection. He was a pain in the ass."

"No surprise there," the Sergeant laughed.

"Yeah, but the problem was the shit fell on me when he failed inspection. The Drill Sergeant chewed me out for not having my squad squared away. And he did that in front of the whole squad."

"Hey, it sucks to be a leader sometimes. How'd that turn out?"

"I laid into him. It was either that too-casual trainee or my head on the block."

"How'd that work out?"

"Not well at all. He blew it off and said the Army was too strict about petty things."

"He didn't care about putting his socks and shorts in the right place, did he?"

"No, he didn't. He said it made no difference in how well he'd do as an MP."

"Well, he sure blew you off. What'd you do?"

"I talked it over with other squad leaders and then talked to the guy one-on-one. Explained what happened to my bunkmate in basic training—a guy who didn't hustle as much as the Drill Sergeant expected during PT."

"Oh?"

"He got a blanket party in the middle of the night."

"Did that change his behavior?"

"For sure! He got a bit more squared away. When everyone else in the platoon heard about the blanket party, they seemed to pick up the pace too."

The Sergeant leaned forward and continued in a low voice, "Okay, that's a good lesson. Now I'll answer your question. I believe three things make for a successful leader. First, I have to grab people's attention in a way that leaves no mistake that I'll kick their ass if they do NOT do what I expect. If leaders don't establish strength initially, lazy guys will be out of control from the get-go. I don't let that happen."

Ben interrupted, "That's what you were doing in the talk the other day, wasn't it? You came across as a hard-ass because you wanted us to know you're someone not to mess with."

"Damn right. I lay the law down early."

"So what's the second thing? Is it what we did this morning?"

"Right. The second thing is to wallop people right away. Like in hockey, you need to thump a guy early if you're going to get respect. Leaders look weak when they talk hard but don't act hard. Then guys view you as a bullshitter, and they won't believe anything you say. Leadership requires that people believe you mean what you say. The sooner that's demonstrated, the more likely people will take you at your word. The quicker you hit someone, the less you need to continue doing it—unless they're just plain stupid."

"So going out to inspect in the morning sends the message that you'll enforce the expectation that we stay alert while on duty."

Sergeant Simon nodded. "Right. In the long run, it's always best to start strong."

"Well, that should do it. Everything should work right after those two actions. What else could be left?"

The Sergeant leaned back with a scowl. "You missed the point, Long. Damn it! I thought you were smart, but you aren't thinking things through. I told you some people come ready, and other people won't show up."

"Oh yeah," Ben sheepishly replied.

"Now you figure it out. Play or get off the field. What's left?"

"You deal with those who don't show up ready?"

"No shit, Sherlock. Damn, I was hoping you were a quicker learner," The Sergeant snarled and leaned forward. "Never let those bastards get away with slacking. You must deal harshly and publicly with anyone who doesn't toe the line."

Ben reflected on his AIT situation and wondered what might have happened next if the trainee failed to comply with pressure.

Sergeant Simon concluded, "The third thing is to quickly and firmly crush those who don't get with the program and stay on track. If you don't address their behavior, they'll undermine team cohesion, and THAT risks mission failure.

*I would've needed to deliver a blanket party to that AIT guy if he hadn't corrected his footlocker.*

"You must eliminate the fuck-ups on your team. You make an example of them in a public way, so everyone sees the consequences of not showing up ready. When you do this hard work early on, it will boost morale."

"Otherwise, all your effort from the first two actions means nothing, and your leader presence shrinks to nothing?"

"Right."

A group of MPs entered the mess hall, and the Sergeant glanced at his watch. "Okay, it's time to get back out there and show everyone who is the boss. I'm stopping in HQ, so meet me at the vehicle in five."

Ben stepped into the bright sunlight and reflected on Sergeant Simon's leadership approach. *I can see how those methods would work in basic training and AIT, but time will tell how well they'll work here.*

# DISGUISES:
## Contrasts in Identity

### April 17, 1970

**The Power of Presence**

"Thank God for the EM Club," declared Greg Pulaski. "I can't spend every night in that barracks. I'm going crazy listening to four kinds of music and those card players arguing."

Bruce Bugliano pulled the tab on a can of beer, and a *whoosh* of air escaped. "This is my favorite sound! Cold beer makes me happy."

"It's too chaotic in the barracks after chow," Ben added. "I can't hear myself think when I'm trying to write a letter."

Bruce laughed, "That's why they invented headphones. Maybe you should spend a little money and get some peace of mind."

"Speaking of peace of mind, how'd your day go with the new boss?" Greg interrupted. "I heard you guys made quite a splash today."

"Yeah," Bruce chimed in. "Sounds like Sergeant Simon wants to ambush guys to catch them off guard. That's bullshit if you ask me."

Ben squirmed in his seat. "I was just his driver, man. I didn't call the shots."

"Some guys are saying you're Simon's favorite," Greg teased.

Ben frowned and snapped, "I didn't volunteer for the job! I don't know why I got assigned to be the supervisor's driver. That's NOT the way I wanted to spend my day."

"Okay, man, relax. We're just having fun with you," Bruce asserted. "But seriously, what was it like? Learn anything useful?"

Ben calmed down and leaned back. "Yeah, I learned things worth knowing."

"Okay, let's hear the inside dope," and Greg set down his beer.

Bruce vigorously nodded, "We want to know everything. That kind of information could help us better prepare to deal with him."

"I spent time in the PMO. A lot's happening there," Ben stated.

"Cut to the chase before I run out of beer," Greg suggested.

"The main thing has to do with how we conduct radio communication. When guys on patrol communicate properly, the supervisor doesn't hassle them. If they don't do it right, Simon comes looking for them."

"What do we need to do to keep him off our backs?" Bruce asked.

"Exactly my point. The radio operator serves as the ears for the Patrol Supervisor. When we check in regularly and report, all's well, the operator dials back to autopilot. But the operator will notify the supervisor if he doesn't hear anything or suspects something's unusual. That's a red flag we don't want to trigger."

"Good to know!" Greg exclaimed. "No one wants the supervisor to come looking for them."

"Roger that," Bruce echoed.

"So that's your PMO insight. What about Simon? What's his deal?" Greg asked.

"Simon isn't the jerk guys make him out to be. All he wants is for everything to run smoothly. He doesn't want to have to deal with trouble, whether it's from the guys or our superiors."

"That sounds like something a suck-up would say," Greg insisted.

"Kinda does sound like it," Bruce agreed.

Ben glared from Greg to Bruce. "It's what I saw!"

"You're gonna have to explain that one," Greg pressed.

"We know what command expects from us while on duty. We should expect we're always on display and living in the spotlight. We must look and act properly, or people will report us."

"For sure," Bruce agreed. "Soldiers, and especially officers, enjoy catching MPs in a uniform violation or goofing off. They use our mistakes to defend their behavior."

Greg's brow furrowed. "What's that got to do with Simon's sneak tactics?"

"Simon believes that checking on guys to see what's really happening is the best way to reduce the reporting of negative behaviors. Otherwise, those reports reflect poorly on his effectiveness as a leader."

"That makes sense," Bruce replied.

"Simon called that leader presence," Ben added. "He said being in the field presents a powerful presence. It's a safety measure because an ounce of prevention saves a pound of cure."

Greg nodded and swallowed the last of his beer.

"You know that's what we do every day on patrol," Ben continued. "Even static posts are a way to demonstrate the power of presence. It's a deterrence. When drivers see MPs, they slow down."

"Okay, I get that," Greg grudgingly admitted.

"So Simon isn't an asshole; he's just trying to avoid trouble?" Bruce asked.

"Right! That's the same thing we're trained as MPs to do," Ben clarified.

## Contrasting Identities

"I guess that helps to explain Simon's behavior, but there are still concerns about you, Ben," Greg challenged.

"Yeah, like who you are and whose side you're on. Guys are worried about working with you. After all, if a guy can't trust his partner . . ." Bruce's voice trailed off.

Ben straightened and slammed his can on the table. "You saying you don't trust me?"

"Not me, man, but other guys are talking," Greg stammered.

"What the fuck, Greg?" Ben shot back. "You know who I am and where I stand. You were with me at the Saigon Zoo and during our guard tower nights. Remember what we did? That's not the behavior of a suck-up who can't be trusted. You know damn well I'm trustworthy. Fuck what those guys say!"

"Hey, I know you're solid, but you got to admit those guys don't know you like I do. You're a stranger, and that's an obstacle to trust."

"That's bullshit."

"Not really, Ben," Bruce interjected. "I don't know you well, and Greg's saying that until you know a guy—"

"Fuck you and those guys too. People shouldn't accuse me of being a suck-up because I'm assigned to drive the supervisor. That's bullshit, and morons like Tucker should have more sense than that."

"I get it, but guys are worried because they don't know who they can trust," Greg interrupted.

"So what happens if Simon picks *you* to be the driver tomorrow? And what if he picks a different guy each day? Then we accuse each other of being a suck-up? We're morons if we fall into that trap. The supervisor gains total control by keeping us divided and mistrusting each other."

"Oh, I didn't think about that," Bruce murmured.

"Obviously! Let's slow down and think this through," Ben advised. "Greg knows I don't fit the police culture profile. My identity is the opposite. My behaviors over the past four months should have made that obvious."

Greg nodded.

"In reality, we sometimes have to live dual identities. I sure wasn't police material before getting drafted, but now I'm serving as an MP. That kind of dramatic change puts some guys in conflict within themselves."

Bruce set his can on the table and leaned forward. "I understand that. Whoever we were before the military, we now have new identities. Our uniform and MP brassard paint us with a distinct identity, whether we're committed to being a bad-ass MP or not."

"That's my point," Ben insisted. "I have to put away my civilian identity and play a role when on patrol."

"That's an interesting way to think about identity," Greg noted. "GIs see our uniform and assume the cover is the book. You're saying we shouldn't assume that what we see is what we'll get?"

"Yes, and I'm a good example," Ben declared. "One day, we're a couple of buddies goofing off on patrol together, and the next day you think I'm a suck-up because I'm the supervisor's driver. Does that make sense?"

"No, not for me. Of course not," Greg replied.

"So, what are you saying?" Bruce asked. "You got multiple identities, and your personal identity is different from your work identity?"

## Camouflage

"That's what I'm saying. I choose the behavior that best keeps me safe where I'm at," Ben explained. "That protects me from unwanted conflicts."

Bruce shook his head. "I couldn't do that. I gotta be who I am."

"I want to avoid unnecessary conflict," Ben continued. "I learned a long time ago that blending in is safer than being perceived as a threat. I let the setting dictate how I behave, and I conceal my personal preferences."

Greg paused and pondered the implications of that scheme. "You think that works? Don't you worry that people will see through your disguise? Guys won't trust you if they suspect you change your behavior to fit the circumstances."

"Maybe, and maybe not," Ben admitted. "If guys understand I'm trying to stay safe, I think they'll accept how I behave."

Bruce looked skeptical. "I don't know about that. It sounds like you're two-faced. I wouldn't know which face I could trust."

"It's a tricky line to walk, and not without risks. But I'd rather be safe than worry about losing friends. If a guy doesn't get why I'm trying to be careful, they probably aren't good friends anyway."

"That's a dangerous game to play," Bruce challenged.

"It depends on who you're dealing with. We interact with three different groups. First, some people only see our on-duty MP face. They're total strangers, and to them, I'm the bad-ass MP. There's no problem with them. The second group is my close friends. They know me well enough to accept the reasons that drive my actions, so there's no problem with them either."

Greg nodded and echoed, "Makes sense."

Ben continued to explain his reasoning. "It's the third group that poses risks. Those are the people who see both sides of my behavior, both the MP face and the personal face. They're confused by my contradictory actions and don't like them. I try to keep that group as small as possible. But they aren't friends, and frankly, their opinions don't matter to me."

"That's harsh," Bruce retorted.

"Sensible, though," Greg interrupted. "You can't please all the people all the time. It's better to be safe. I'm with Ben on that one."

"Which group does Simon belong to?" Bruce asked.

"The first, hopefully," Ben laughed.

"No shit!" Greg added. "You hope he never sees both those identities. If he does, you're fucked."

"You better be careful," Bruce warned. "He's a smart guy, and if he sees through your disguise, there'll be hell to pay. How do you think you're going to get away with fooling him?"

## Disguises

"Blending into a non-friendly environment is a vital life skill," Greg interrupted. "Disguises use camouflage to fool predators from recognizing you as prey. Ben hopes Simon won't see him either as a threat or victim."

"Is that right, Ben?" Bruce asked. "What did you do, and how'd it work today?"

Ben cautiously glanced around the EM Club, leaned forward, and whispered, "The key is to understand what people expect and give it to them. After hearing what Simon said in the platoon meeting, I had some thoughts about his priorities. Simon wants guys to listen to him and respect his experience and insights. I also believe he expects people will appreciate his leadership style and want to learn from him."

"That's pretty basic stuff, and it could apply to lots of people. My question was, what did *you* do? How'd it work?" Bruce persisted.

"I wore the disguise he wanted to see," Ben stated. "I figured the reason I got the driver assignment was to allow him to size me up. He was looking for a specific attitude and behavior, and I decided to play that character."

"You're talking over my head!" Bruce snapped. "Explain it like a regular guy. No more of your fancy college mumbo jumbo."

Ben noticed Greg's cocked eyebrow. *I guess I'm dancing around the answer.*

"Sorry. Here's the point. I behaved like a super suck-up. I treated Simon like he was the smartest leader I've ever met and asked questions that made him think I wanted to learn everything I could so I could grow up to be just like him."

"Aha!" Bruce declared. "You *are* a suck-up, just like the guys said."

Ben squinted and glared at Bruce. "Haven't you heard a word I said?! If you think that, then fuck you. And I don't give a shit what you think. My goal is to be sure Simon thinks I'm a great MP and a promotable guy he can trust. If he sees me that way, my life will run a whole lot smoother. And if the cost is that a few knuckleheads think I'm a suck-up who can't be trusted, that's a price I'm willing to pay."

"So, you're as bad as Tucker said you were?" Bruce asked.

Greg interrupted, "No, man, that's not the case. You have to look at the big picture. Simon's a hard-ass, and he's going to break balls if you're not with the program. All Ben's doing is staying on Simon's good side and hoping that helps keep Simon's heat from coming down on him. Any smart guy would do the same thing."

"I'm no suck-up. Are you saying I'm stupid?" Bruce barked.

Greg shook his head in disbelief. "Geez, maybe you've had one too many beers, brother. He's saying those disguises are a tactic to stay safe, just like camouflage. Ben's behavior has nothing to do with being a suck-up. It's about being street-smart. Think of it like going undercover."

"I don't like Simon's style, and I don't want him to think I'm his boy," Bruce persisted.

"Do you want Simon to zero in on you and make your life miserable?" Greg asked.

"I can take it!" Bruce exclaimed. "He's not that tough."

"Okay, whatever. To each, his own," and Greg threw up his hands. "Maybe we've had enough for tonight. Tomorrow's another day. Who knows, maybe you'll draw supervisor driver duty. Then you can take your stand."

"And I will. Just watch," and Bruce slammed his can down.

"Good luck with that," Greg countered and pushed away from the table.

Ben reflected on the rising tension over the difference in the viewpoints. *This conversation sure went in the ditch! I never expected that being assigned the supervisor's driver would end up there. Simon may be a lot smarter than we think.*

# UNEXPECTED VISIT:
## Rendezvous

## April 19, 1970

### Reminiscence

"A day off, this is a treat!" Randy DeMarco exclaimed between bites. "Any plans for today?"

"Nothing special! Probably just listen to music, read a book, and write letters," Ben replied as he pushed away his tray.

"Mail call is soon. Maybe you'll get something from your wife."

"That anticipation feels like the worst part of the day. I'm anxious about what'll come, but letters from family and friends seem to be few and far between nowadays. But when I do receive letters, especially from my wife, it's the best day."

"I've seen that effect. Lots of guys try to act casual about mail call; being disappointed is worse than expecting nothing."

"I'm a good example of that problem. When I'm itching to receive something, and it doesn't arrive, I'm the last person you want to be around. When I don't get mail, I can get ornery."

"Yes, I've seen that too. Sometimes you're angry, even hostile."

"Yeah, my mood can swing low or high," Ben confessed.

"Guys like me without wives or girlfriends are well aware of that! We can set our watches by how quickly you married guys storm off to the EM Club to drown your sorrows. It's almost as predictable as the afternoon monsoon."

Ben shook his head. "I'll bet watching married guy's emotional swings make you thankful you don't have a girl at home."

"I do admit the thought has crossed my mind. Going without is easier than aching every day for a letter and then sinking into a funk when you don't get one. It looks like marriage can be a stone around a guy's neck, at least over here."

Ben paused, lost in thought. "You remember the training songs about Jody (a reference to a man at home who steals the girl of a serviceman)?"

"Sure, who could forget the ultimate blues for enlisted men!"

"When you're married or have a girlfriend, that fear always sits in the back of your mind, you know? A guy can work himself into a frenzy worrying about what's distracted her from writing.

"You're right. I'm glad I don't have that worry hanging over my head!"

Ben nodded and glanced at his watch.

"Guess it's time, huh?"

"Almost."

"Let's get this over with! I'll go with you."

Ben hoped to receive mail from Sue but instead received a letter from Tom Mueller, a high school friend serving in Vietnam.

Randy looked quizzically at the envelope. "Did you expect that? Who's this guy?"

"This is a surprise! I knew Tom re-upped and was serving a second tour, but how bizarre is it to get a letter? I didn't know you could write a letter from in-country. How did he get my address?"

"Don't keep me in suspense. What'd he say? Is he all right?"

Ben skimmed the scrawled letter. "Tom's stationed in the I Corps near the DMZ. He's flying to Saigon on business and wants to visit me here in Long Binh. Holy shit, he's arriving today! What a coincidence that today's one of my rare non-duty days."

"Wow, he must be a great friend to do that."

"We've been friends a while. We weren't close in high school, but we were together in a third classmate's car on Memorial Day 1966 when a drunk driver broadsided our vehicle. That was a near-fatal accident for me, and I was hospitalized for seven days. Tom was injured, too, so the accident led to a survivors' bond between us."

"I've heard that traumatic experiences will do that to people."

"It sure did for us. Tom visited me out of the blue a year ago when I was still in college. We hadn't seen each other in over two years because he volunteered for the Army in 1967."

"What motivated him to visit?"

"He was on leave from his first tour when he heard I was about to be drafted. He shared stories about defusing mines as an Explosive Ordnance Detachment specialist (EOD)."

Randy's brow furrowed. "Was that supposed to be a pep talk?"

"I think he just wanted to make a personal connection. Maybe he figured I'd end up in Vietnam? Despite the risks, or perhaps because of them, he reenlisted for a second tour."

"Wow! He's some kind of hardcore guy!"

"He always was intense," Ben laughed.

"Was that the last time you saw him?"

"No, he visited again unexpectedly the night before I left for Vietnam and offered timely advice. It meant a lot to me that he took the time to show support before I shipped out." (See 1st Moon: Innocence, Story 1 ~ Last Day of Home).

They parted ways, and Ben returned to the hooch. *Tom's become a steadfast friend. I bet this trip from Quang Tri and the detour to Long Binh required a lot of finagling to arrange. This visit isn't a lucky coincidence. He looked out for me before and probably wants to see for himself that I'm doing okay.*

## Unexpected Rendezvous

Ben waited all morning, wondering if Tom would show up. It was nearly 1:00 p.m. when the company clerk strolled into the hooch. "Long, you got a visitor at HQ. Come sign him in. He claims he caught a military flight from Quang Tri to Saigon MACV and a truck to Long Binh. It seems a stretch that an enlisted guy has that much pull."

"It's true. Tom's with EOD up north. He sent a letter from there."

Ben stepped into HQ, and the sight of Tom standing before him was as striking as the blast in his face from the air-conditioning. A stream of memories rushed across his mind, ranging from high school antics to the accident and countless hours of drinking and talking.

"Holy shit, you're really here!" Ben yelled.

"Of course! I told you I'd make it down here," Tom declared, flashing a sheepish grin that left Ben unsure of his sincerity. "What're you saying? You didn't think I'd show up?"

Tom's remark resurrected a truth-or-bullshit thought, but Ben didn't want to start their visit on the wrong foot. "No, man! It's just an expression. I'm stunned that you're here. *Wow!*"

"So, you gonna sign me in? You know I don't have good memories of MPs, and standing here is beginning to give me the heebie-jeebies."

Ben wondered how much of that story might be true. "I can believe you probably did get in trouble with the MPs. And now you're in the lair of the beast. Nothing to worry about unless you're AWOL, of course."

Tom's grin disappeared, and Ben decided to fuck with him some more. He turned toward the clerk and asked, "Did you check his pass?"

"No, I thought he was your friend."

"Yeah, you're right. Let's cut the guy some slack."

"But I could if you insist," the clerk continued.

Ben turned toward Tom. "Come on, let's get out of here before they find any outstanding warrants."

Not amused, Tom snarled, "You're letting the cop thing go to your head. Don't forget it's us EOD guys who keep your convoys from getting blown to shit on the road."

"Right. We'd better take care of each other. What do you say we get a beer and a burger?"

They stepped out of HQ into the blazing heat, and Ben continued, "It's great that you could get down here, man. I appreciate it."

"Hey, I was going to be in the neighborhood anyway and thought I'd drop in to check on you. Our company had documents that needed to be delivered to MACV, and I volunteered to be the courier. It's hard to get out of the bush, and Saigon is too sweet a trip to pass up. Hell, after that distance, Long Binh is just a short hop up the highway."

They settled into a corner of the EM Club and ordered food and drink. "Here's to meeting friends in strange places," Ben declared as they tapped their cans in a toast.

"Fuck that. Here's to both of us getting home alive," Tom countered.

"I'll drink to that all night," Ben seconded, and they chugged their beers.

"That's refreshing. It reminds me of old times."

"So, how's your second tour?

Tom set his can down. "You know, after the first tour, it gets a lot easier. I gotta tell you; there were times in the first go-round I thought I was a goner."

"I can't imagine what that's like."

A shadow crossed over Tom's face. "I'm not in the field as much this tour. When I am, it's supervising cherries instead of digging mines out. Even when I'm in the mud, I've got a lot more skill after twelve months of handling explosives."

"I suppose there's no teacher like experience."

"Even though it gets easier, I have to fight the tendency to treat it like it's a routine duty. Any of those mines could send me home in a bag."

Ben stood and offered, "I'll get the next round. We're going to need another. Talking about dying is an instant buzz kill."

"Life's too short; let's drink faster."

Ben returned with two more cold ones.

"So, how's life as an MP?" Tom asked.

Ben spent the next forty-five minutes recounting his in-country experiences. He highlighted the dullness of port security contrasted with the wildness of Saigon's bars, drugs, and black-market temptations.

"If I didn't know all that was true, I'd accuse you of making shit up. Those stories sound like tales from a sordid novel," Tom laughed.

"To anyone who hasn't experienced it, I suppose it does come across like crazy bullshit. As the saying goes, you had to be there."

"Don't worry, brother, I believe you. This country's fucked up. The villages around us are too dangerous to enter, but the same prostitution and black market shit happens everywhere. I bet soldiers with money support the same business opportunities wherever they go."

"Yeah, extra cash in a GI's pocket seems to attract criminal enterprises."

"How about your duty? Are you running convoys? Convoys up north always include armed MPs in combat gear. We're getting the shit kicked out of us every few days with ambushes. And when that's not happening, we have to clear road mines."

"Our company runs convoys at night, but my platoon patrols the highway on days. Base command says it's supposed to be like Stateside MP duty, but it's nothing like patrolling on a Stateside base."

Tom interrupted with a laugh, "Command always seems to get it wrong because they see life from a distance. It's hard for officers to understand what's real when they sit behind a desk in a fortified compound."

"Suppose that's true everywhere, huh? Reality is something else. We're patrolling a major highway, and the traffic is mostly Vietnamese vehicles. A lot of our days have us dealing with accidents."

"Yes, I've seen their crazy driving. It's like the Vietnamese don't have any sense, or worse, don't care."

"Right. We've been at the scene of a few ugly crashes lately," Ben sighed.

"What about home? You're married now. How's that going?"

"Yeah, married and more. I've got a son now. He's three months old."

"Three months? You mean since you got in-country?"

"Right. Great way to start a family, isn't it?"

"That sucks, man. I'm sorry. I don't know how I'd handle Nam with a wife and kid back in the world. That's a bitch. You must be pretty fucked up over it."

"I try not to dwell on it. That's especially important now that I'm patrolling the highway instead of sitting in a secure port facility. It's not safe to think about them too much because the distraction puts me at risk. It's important I focus my attention on the here and now."

Their food arrived, interrupting the emotionally charged subject. Ben chewed his burger and mindlessly stared at the television on the wall, hoping the image would distract them from restarting the topic. *I don't want to talk about home stuff and let it mess with my head.*

Tom looked at the television and also pretended it was worthy of attention.


## Volunteers, Draftees, and Dodgers

They finished eating in silence and ordered a third beer.

Tom finally spoke. "Ever hear from Paul?"

"Not really. Once I got a letter from him telling me how bad the Vietnam war is and how I should've gone to Canada."

"Great friend!" Tom snapped sarcastically. "He always acted like he was smarter than everyone else. What the hell does he know?"

"Paul was blunt in his letter. His anti-war attitude's pretty strong. He wrote I was stupid for going along with the draft."

Tom interrupted, "Here we are in Vietnam getting our asses shot at, and he sits at home enjoying his freedom and criticizing our willingness to fight for it. Fuck him. And where is he anyway—protected behind his student deferment at some second-rate college?"

"I'm sure he has a student deferment. That what college guys get."

"He thinks guys should go to Canada. I'd like to see him over here!"

Ben stared across the table at Tom, unsure how to respond.

"Let me say this," Tom continued. "When I visited you at college, I thought you didn't support the war, but you respected me for my decision to volunteer."

"Of course I did, Tom."

"Good! I expect that from you with both our dads being veterans of WWII."

"Yeah, and they both are pretty fucked up from it, based on how much they drink," Ben added.

"Well, there's a price for everything."

"I don't want this war, but I respect a guy for the decision he believes he needs to make. I respect you for choosing to volunteer, but I have to respect Paul for his anti-war position, too."

"That's where we disagree, man. I respect you for being anti-war, but you still accepted your duty to serve when drafted. What bothers me isn't so much that someone's anti-war, but to suggest you leave the country rather than serve when called. I just can't stomach that," Tom emphatically stated.

"We're getting intense here, aren't we? We're sitting in Vietnam arguing about guys back in the world as if they matter. It doesn't make a shit's difference here. Why should we give a damn about other people's political views?"

"Because their actions support the enemy. Anti-war assholes are providing aid and comfort to the Vietcong. We are kicking Charlie's ass, but anti-war protests reinforce the enemy's resolve to keep fighting a losing war, hoping we'll eventually quit and go home."

"This war's all but over," Ben insisted. "We've already won in every way that counts. I don't see how protests will change that fact."

"Well, one thing's for fucking sure – I'd rather have you covering my back than any of those assholes! They're not guys I could trust as a partner."

## No Room for Feelings

"Well, we play the cards we're dealt, don't we? I would have liked to keep my student deferment, but I'm here in Vietnam. Whatever happens, I've accepted my duty. Besides, I didn't get here by accident. I deserved my draft notice by doing so poorly in school," Ben confessed.

"That's my point. You're not afraid to accept responsibility. Hell, you extended your tour, didn't you? You're a guy with a wife and kid, and yet you're willing to serve an extra seventy-five days in Nam."

"That's some kind of fucked-up logic, isn't it? I get drafted, and then I volunteer for more Vietnam. Guess that makes me a volunteering draftee?"

"Man, once a guy gets over here, we're all volunteers. Every patrol puts us on the line. We either step up or back away from the responsibilities. Most guys do their job as best they can. That's stepping up in my book."

Ben stared at the table and squeezed his empty can.

"You got a wife and kid, Ben. That's a hell of a responsibility and an added emotional burden. I can't imagine how that weighs on you, even if you do try to keep it out of your mind. The only thing I can think is it must put an ass-kicking heartache into every day."

Ben looked up and pleaded, "Let's not go there. It's best I keep the family and Vietnam in separate boxes. If they come together, especially while I'm in-country, there's no telling what bad decisions I'll make. I can't afford to let those feelings distract me."

"Sure, man. I respect you for what you have to do. Fuck this place anyway." Tom stood and added, "It's been great seeing you. My time's up, and I need to catch a flight. One thing's for sure—never take your friends or your life for granted."

Ben watched Tom weave toward the bathroom and reflected on their surreal interaction. *Who would expect that someone from high school could just show up as a visitor in a place like this? Vietnam—what a crazy place.*

Tom returned and repeated, "I've got to leave, but it's been great catching up with you. We're having a hell of an adventure over here, and it's more bearable when you know there are people like you and me doing the work."

Ben started to respond, but Tom held up his hand. "Don't get emotional with me, man. You've explained the situation with your wife and kid very well, and I agree with you. Let's just walk away and appreciate we had this chance to connect. I love you like a brother, but there's no room for feelings in Vietnam. If we're both lucky, maybe we'll see each other back in the world someday."

**Letter Home 127:** *April 19, 1970; 2045 hours*

*Dearest Sue:*

*I love you.*

*I hope the reason you are not writing is not because I have not been, because it is not my fault. I've had no time here to do much more than work, sleep, and eat. It is good in a way though, because time flies.*

*I've learned a lot about jeep in the last couple of days because I've spent time in the Motor Pool trying to keep them in shape.*

*I really can't think of anything to say, but R & R will be wonderful because my mind daydreams about it all the time. Fifty-two days!*

*I hope the rest of our time apart (9 months) is not as bad as the last month. There is nothing I need more now than you and your love, and getting few letters really hurts.*

*I'm especially sad today because a friend from high school showed up here. He is in his second tour and I think Vietnam has made him a bit crazy. I don't know maybe he was like that before and I didn't notice it!? All I know is I talked to him for two hours and realized he is a complete opposite of me.*

*Maybe it is me, after all, Tom told me I had ruined my life. He even said he felt sorry because I was dumb enough to get married. Some people don't know what it means to be loved and love.*

*Please send me several pictures of yourself, I got enough of Johnny, especially since all babies look alike to me. I guess I'll make a poor doctor.*

*I love you, angel. Keep my love because it can't survive by itself.*

*All my love for the woman I love,*

*Ben*

# EXPLORATION:
# The Brick Factory

## April 20, 1970

### Uneasy Partners

"Patrol Bravo One! Bugliano and Long!" Sergeant Simon barked at the men assembled in guard mount.

*Yep, saw that on the duty roster. Today should be interesting.*

The Sergeant continued the roster review and closed with his usual instruction. "Men, today we expect you to stay sharp. Safety is your number one priority. Be focused, be professional, and take care of each other. Dismissed!"

The men moved to their vehicles as Bruce Bugliano walked up to Ben. "Long, I'm the senior MP, and I've decided you'll drive today."

"Roger that. I knew you had more time in grade, so I got the vehicle from the motor pool. We're ready to go."

"Good. Let's get on the road." They placed their weapons and go-bags into the jeep.

Ben drove out of the company area toward the base's main gate. He turned south on the highway and methodically shifted to accelerate to forty-five miles per hour. "Since our AO extends from QL-15 to Thu Duc, how about we make a run to Thu Duc and visit each checkpoint on the way back?"

"Good idea. It sounds like you've done this before."

"This may be our first time as partners, but this isn't my first rodeo."

"Let's get one thing straight. I'm in charge, and I'll decide where we go and when we do it," Bruce insisted.

"You're the boss; I'm the driver," Ben affirmed.

"And don't forget it."

"So, you still don't trust me because of the Simon thing?"

"I heard your explanation at the EM Club, but I'm withholding judgment until I see for myself."

"Okay, that's fine, but maybe you're on trial today, too. After all, how do I know you aren't a suck-up disguised as a regular guy?" Ben laughed.

"Fuck you, Long."

"I'm just stating the obvious. That bullshit cuts both ways."

"There's the Thu Duc intersection. Turn around and head toward SP-14," Bruce directed.

"Roger that."

They rode in silence for the next ten minutes. Ben braked hard and eased onto the dirt trail a hundred yards south of SP-14. He slowed to a crawl to navigate the rutted path up the ridge. The MPs in the static post watched as Bravo One approached.

"Guess it's hard to surprise you guys," Bruce asserted.

"No shit," Frank Succors declared. "We saw your dust long before we recognized your friendly faces. You can't sneak up on us when you have to drive so damn slow on that rocky two-track."

"You guys looked like a couple of bobble-heads," Randy DeMarco laughed.

Ben agreed, "I thought we were going to get shaken out of our seats!"

The four MPs exchanged small talk for a few minutes when Bruce announced, "We'll come back later; right now we got to check on SP-16."

Ben started the engine and descended the northern two-track path, equally as rough as the southern trail. "If I go any faster, we'll get whiplash."

"No hurry, we don't want injuries from reckless driving."

They traveled a few miles north and eased onto the shoulder at SP-16.

"Well, look at these two working together!" Greg Pulaski exclaimed. "You make quite an odd pair of partners."

"I'll bet these two will be going at each other's throats before the day is over," Tucker Bronson added. "I'd love to be there to hear it when it happens."

Ben glared at Tucker but remained silent.

"I'm in charge, and things will run just fine today," Bruce stated. "You two enjoy your sunbathing."

Ben glanced at Bruce. *It sounds like maybe he didn't appreciate that comment. I wonder if he doesn't like Tucker.*

"Cross the bridge and then turn around to make another run south to Thu Duc," Bruce directed, waving toward the Dong Nai River.

Ben pulled away from SP-16, aggressively merged into traffic, and accelerated toward the bridge. At mid-span, they passed Sergeant Simon's patrol vehicle heading south. Each waved as they moved in opposite directions.

Bruce grabbed the radio mic and reported Bravo One's position and status. He turned to Ben and commented, "I remember what you said about routine check-ins. That was good advice about keeping the PMO informed so they won't think they need to pay extra attention to us. Maintaining a high profile on the radio will make it easier to stay under the radar."

"I like how you think."

"Well, at least there's one thing we agree on."

They crossed the bridge, sped through the QL-15 intersection at the base's southwest corner, and pulled a U-turn. Heading south, they waved as they raced past SP-16 and SP-14. They passed Sergeant Simon's vehicle again at the water filtration plant near Thu Duc. "Looks like he's finished his morning inspections and is returning to the PMO," Ben remarked.

"That's good news for us, right? Simon saw us twice, and both those positions matched our radio check-in reports. Now he should feel comfortable that he knows where we are and that we're properly conducting patrol. Hopefully, he'll leave us alone if your theory about his behavior is right."

"I'm right, and we should be good now. Simon's not interested in doing more work. He wants a quiet, smooth day. Once he's confident that everything's going well, he'll be content to spend most of the afternoon in the PMO. We're following the saying: Render unto Caesar what is Caesar's."

"Works for me," Bruce nodded.

"By the way, did you notice those roads leading east from the highway? Do you think we should check any of them out so we can see what's on the other side of the tree line?"

"I saw them. The one I was curious about was the road behind SP-16. It looks like the area opens up behind those buildings."

Their morning passed quickly and without incident. They conducted several patrol loops of the AO, including regular stops at the two static posts. They also radioed the other two mobile patrols and rendezvoused where the AOs overlapped.

## Back Channel

Ben and Bruce entered the mess hall at eleven thirty for chow. They moved through the line, eyeing the unappetizing choices. They noticed Sergeant Simon seated with his driver and decided the smart move would be to join them.

"How's your day going?" the Sergeant asked.

"Calm and smooth," Bruce replied. "No accidents this morning."

"That's the way we like it. I appreciate your professionalism. You demonstrate excellent radio protocol. You stay mobile but regularly connect with your posts and the other patrols. That shows great teamwork."

"We know what they expect us to do," Ben acknowledged. Bruce nodded in agreement.

Ben and Bruce finished up and returned to the road to relieve each of the static posts for their lunch breaks.

Bruce broke the silence. "Sitting on a checkpoint for a while is relaxing after hours in that frenzied traffic."

"Yeah, I hate doing static post duty for twelve hours, but an hour in the middle of the day isn't too bad."

"A whole day of observation kills me. It's like dying from boredom."

Ben pointed toward the trail behind SP-16 that disappeared behind the buildings. "Maybe we can check out that road later?"

"Let's see what these guys say. We can't do it unless they cover our asses."

Greg and Tucker returned from chow, and the four men discussed exploring the road to discover what was behind their position.

"You said earlier you wondered what's there," and Bruce pointed toward the buildings behind the checkpoint.

"Right. It makes me a little uneasy," Tucker confirmed.

"We can check it out, but we'll need your help."

"We can't do anything anchored to this position," Greg protested.

"You can cover for us," Ben chimed in.

Greg furrowed his brow. "How?"

"Ever use back channels?" Ben asked.

"Huh?" Tucker mumbled.

"Like this," and Ben reached toward the radio and twisted knobs. Loud static followed by chatter in Vietnamese startled them.

"What'd you do?" Tucker asked.

"This switch changes frequencies. Turn the knob two notches, and you're on a different frequency. Nobody else knows what frequency you're using. The new frequency is usually vacant or used by ARVNs. If we both make the same change and keep our conversation to a minimum, without identifiers, we can be connected. The PMO won't be aware that something's happening."

"Genius!" Greg exclaimed. "How'd you learn that?"

"Figured it out while I was in the PMO. That's another one of the many benefits of being the supervisor's driver." Ben frowned and glared at Tucker.

"Okay, maybe something good came out of being Simon's driver," Tucker conceded.

"Sounds like that plan might work. What's next?" Greg asked.

"We'll make another run to Thu Duc and stop at SP-14 to maintain high-visibility. Then we'll cross this bridge again before we return here. We'll also give a couple of radio updates about our activity. I think all that visibility will give us a window of time for exploring that trail," Bruce explained.

The men agreed, and Brave One headed south toward Thu Duc.


## The Brick Factory

They returned an hour later to SP-16 and reviewed the back-channel communication process. "Let's be sure we stay low-key," Ben encouraged.

"What do you mean?" Greg asked.

"We'll use a keyword as the signal to switch frequencies. We'll pick a phrase that nobody will notice, like 'a pretty dusty day' as the keyword."

"That's a normal-sounding phrase," Tucker agreed.

"Right. The second rule is we won't use the keyword except in an emergency. There's no reason to do a frequency change unless we're in trouble. If things go okay, we'll never use the signal."

"Minimum use means it'll be available when we need it," Bruce added.

They all agreed, and Bravo One eased along the trail to the east. Immediately after they passed the three-story buildings, the patrol emerged in open landscape.

"Take it slow, Ben," Bruce cautioned. "We'd better watch the road."

"Got it! I'm focused on staying in the ruts. We don't want to run over anything and disable our vehicle."

They moved slowly on the trail and watched the bordering rice paddies. In a hundred yards, they arrived at an intersecting road. "Which way?" Ben asked.

"The river is on our left, and that might be a dead end. Let's turn right and travel south. That'll keep us parallel to the highway."

Ben eased the vehicle onto the new trail, a wider road to accommodate two ox carts. His sweaty palms slid on the steering wheel as he spotted a cluster of thatched huts. Ben slowed for a more careful look and reached into his go-bag for the camera.

"What're you doing?" Bruce demanded. "Do you think you're a tourist?"

"As long as we've come this far, I might as well take pictures. Who knows if we'll ever be here again? I want to remember what I've seen."

"You're crazy," Bruce protested, shaking his head.

"Look, nobody's shooting. Hell, nobody's even around," Ben explained as he pointed toward the huts.

"Bullshit. I saw a guy over there, and there could be more watching us," Bruce argued as he also pointed toward the same huts.

"We're MPs. They're not going to fuck with us. They think we're on a recon mission. If we act like we're searching the area, they'll lay low."

Bruce gripped the M-16 resting between his knees.

Ben eased forward, stopped, and shot pictures for fifty yards. He captured half a dozen images of the huts. Most were thatched, but some were covered with corrugated steel panels similar to those he'd seen on Saigon's roadside shanties. They spotted a few Vietnamese, but each person either stepped back into the foliage or scurried into their dwelling.

"See how that woman hurried away and the men stepped behind trees? They aren't going to confront us. Hell, they hope we don't even see them."

"What's that mean?" Bruce asked.

"We're the fucking police and the last people they want to meet. It wouldn't surprise me to find out these civilians are friendlier to Charlie than to the South Vietnam government."

"Doesn't that make it more dangerous for us to drive slowly past them?"

"Not during the day. They're worried we're trolling – you know, trying to bait them. They probably suspect we have helicopters waiting to swoop in and waste them as soon as they show any hostility," Ben explained.

"We should keep moving instead of stopping for pictures!"

"The truth is we're safer by moving slowly and acting cocky. Our behavior shows we're looking for somebody, and none of them want to be caught. Most Vietnamese fear the police and try to stay out of our way. To them, we're dangerous."

Bruce paused to ponder that scenario. "What makes you think that?"

"I spent time around the White Mice in Saigon and studied their behaviors. Their tactics, and the civilians' reactions, led me to think there's a climate of police intimidation here. After years of harsh police aggression, many civilians have developed anxiety and fear about them."

They reached another open area bordered by rice paddies, and Bruce relaxed his grip on the rifle.

"Look ahead!" Ben directed. "I see a cluster of larger buildings."

"Shit, what's that?" Bruce exclaimed and tightened his grip again on the rifle.

A three-story brick building topped with an expansive sheet metal roof occupied the center of the compound. As Ben inched the jeep forward, he spotted several more buildings with piles of large logs and stacks of neatly arranged bricks strewn along the side.

"That's strange," Bruce declared.

"Yeah!" Ben echoed. "And no people either! That's even stranger."

They dismounted and approached one of the buildings for a closer look. "Look there!" Ben pointed toward the side wall shaded by a sheet metal overhang. "Those oval openings are oven doors. This building's a large furnace with six openings on each side."

"That explains those piles of logs," Bruce concluded.

"And, of course, those stacks of bricks."

"Who would've expected to find a brick furnace out here?"

"It's a surprise, that's for sure. But I guess all that's needed to make bricks are trees and clay," Ben added. He snapped pictures of the buildings, log piles, and kilns.

They returned to the jeep and drove a few dozen yards farther until they reached another open area where rows of bricks lie curing, covered by sheet metal panels. Ben shot another picture. "Those rows look fifty feet long."

"What are you now, a freelancer for *National Geographic* magazine?" Bruce teased.

"It's fascinating! This is basic industrial stuff. Besides, a picture is worth a thousand words. No one will believe our story without proof."

"You're crazy. Has anyone ever told you that?"

## Normal Lives

"Shush, listen," Ben whispered.

Bruce cocked his head and shrugged his shoulders.

"I hear Vietnamese," Ben whispered more softly.

Ben unhooked his holster flap and eased slowly forward past the corner of the next building. "There's another brick drying yard and a dozen men at work. They must have noticed us, but they're continuing to work."

"I guess we finally found the workers," Bruce stated.

"We knew somebody had to be here. Bricks don't bake themselves."

"Funny guy! Keep moving. We've spent enough time here."

Ben accelerated quickly past the brick-making compound. "Well, this has been interesting. Everything we've seen is normal enough, wouldn't you say?"

"Yeah, normal lives for abnormal people."

"Hey, these are normal people trying to live their lives."

"They're gooks, and I don't trust any of them!" Bruce shot back.

Ben decided silence would prevent an argument. *Geez, these are just regular people trying to make a living. Everybody here isn't Vietcong. We're looking at ordinary life that's been going on for centuries and will continue long after we're gone.*

"There's a Vietnamese truck loaded with bricks. Let's follow it. I bet it's headed toward the highway," Bruce instructed.

"Makes sense. A truck with that heavy load needs a solid road."

They caught up with the slow-moving truck, and Ben followed behind rather than attempt to pass on an unfamiliar narrow road. Within a mile, they arrived at the highway.

"I was right! That brick truck came out to the highway," Bruce crowed.

"Right. We're at the gasoline alley area." Ben gunned the engine to merge into heavy traffic heading north. They reached SP-16 in a few minutes and pulled up alongside the other jeep.

"How'd it go? You guys weren't gone that long. And how did you end up coming back from the south instead of returning the way you went?" Tucker asked in a rapid string of questions.

Bruce recapped their journey through the back country, emphasizing his annoyance at Ben's slow driving and shooting pictures of thatched huts. He grew more animated when he described the brick furnace and crowed proudly about his idea to follow the track to the highway.

"Sounds like quite an adventure," Greg remarked.

"Now you've got something on Long if he ever tries to rat on you," Tucker added with a wink.

"Relax, Tucker. Today was a good day, and I'm okay with Ben. He's a decent guy, like you and me. After what we did today, I'm comfortable trusting him. You'll have to figure that out for yourself, but I'm fine with him as a partner," Bruce declared.

*Brick Furnace*

*Brick Oven*

*Brick Drying*

*Brick Yard*

**Letter Home 128:** *April 21, 1970; Time – (Not noted)*

*Dearest Angel:*

*I love you. Tonight I am so uptight I'm going wild. I'm ready to climb the walls and scream. Please buy the Beatles' Abbey Road Album – Carry That Weight is a heavy song for me.*

*I've read today's paper and all the news tears my soul from my body. University of Wisconsin has riots, Cambodia is in flames, United States involvement in Laos is finally disclosed (to surprise of people but not me).*

*God, Sue, I am so helpless here. A revolution is starting in the U.S. and I can't even help. A World War is starting in Southeast Asia and I'm a slave of the American imperialist war machine.*

*Maybe I've gotten too involved about not being involved, but I need your help. I'd like to go AWOL now but I know better. I'd like to move to Canada after I finish college but I don't know. I don't want my son to live in a burning and dying nation.*

*If I don't write a book I am a fool.*

*I cannot believe the Senate and all those fool conservatives want to impeach Supreme Court Douglas for Points of Rebellion, he wrote the same thing Thomas Jefferson wrote! I'll bet they'd try to impeach Jefferson too!*

*This government is so sick I feel it should be changed or dissolved.*

*Help me angel – I need to know if I'm crazy or right in my thoughts, because they are so powerful in my mind. I'm still alive, and I feel my mind is still in touch with you darling, so don't get upset.*

*This is an answer to your request to tell you my problem – here it is in a nutshell – your husband thinks.*

*God, I need peace. If I had you near me Sue, I could live with the ugliness of reality, but alone I can see nothing but sadness.*

*All my soul,*

*Ben*

*I Love You!!!*

# CONCRETE ACTION: Shelter

## April 22, 1970

### Special Detail

Ben looked forward to the day, not minding too much the same bland breakfast. "This is one of those rare days when I'm not scheduled for duty."

"Lucky you!" Tucker Bronson replied. "I usually work ten to twelve days straight."

"Even when I'm not on the duty roster, I sometimes get posted to duty to replace someone who reported for sick call."

"Well, you should know in half an hour. I've got to get to guard mount."

Ben finished chow and headed back to the hooch. *The patrol teams are assembled and ready to roll out soon. Hopefully, I'll finally get some free time.*

He pulled a bundle of letters and a pad from the footlocker. *I've fallen behind in connecting with the world since my transfer. It's been a while since I've had uninterrupted time. Maybe I can catch up on correspondence with family and friends.*

He hunched over the footlocker and frowned at his bed. *Comfortable furniture isn't available in the Army, so my footlocker will have to do for a desk. This saggy bunk is the closest thing I have for a chair. But I'm not going to complain. I've heard some units only have hammocks for sleeping.*

With everyone on duty, Ben relished the solitude of the hooch. He reread letters that recently arrived. *I'm behind in answering everyone! It's tough to prioritize. After I finish this letter to Sue, I'm not sure who I should write to next.*

He examined an in-country envelope and recalled Tom's visit a few days earlier. *It sure was a surprise to see Tom, but a positive one. I'll write a quick note to thank him.* He grabbed a pen and started to write. Out of the corner of his eye, he thought someone moved close by. *That's probably the hooch girl. I'm not going to let her interrupt me.*

The sound of a man's voice startled him, and he twisted to make eye contact.

"Glad to find you, Long!" Sergeant Bruffer exclaimed. "I hoped you were in the area. We have an important job, and I'm recruiting help."

*Is he asking for my help, or is this the Army way of telling me I just volunteered?*

"Hey, Sergeant, what's up?" Ben mumbled.

## Preparing for Monsoons

"We have a simple job that needs to get done today. How about you come with me?" the Sergeant asked with a smirk used by people with power, who know they're not asking a question.

"Oh, man. Today's my first day off in a long time, and I have all these letters to answer," Ben protested.

"Cut the bullshit! You'll have plenty of time for letters after you take care of the Army's priorities. Of course, that depends on how fast you get your ass up and take care of business. Now get the fuck over to HQ! We're putting a work detail together, and you're on it."

The Sergeant didn't wait for a response and walked out of the hooch.

Ben stared after the Sergeant until out of sight. *He knows full well he doesn't need me to agree. There're a lot of things I'd like to tell that ass, but none are safe. Anything I say won't matter and will probably dig a hole that'll make my day worse. I'm in the Army—they own me. No point in arguing because there's no way to win.*

He placed his letters and paper back into the footlocker, pulled on his fatigue jacket, and headed toward HQ. Three other men stood with Sergeant Bruffer, and they all looked pissed off.

"Wait here – I'll be right back," Bruffer ordered.

*Great, now we're playing the Army game of hurry up and wait.*

With the Sergeant out of sight, Dave Hernandez spoke up first. "Looks like we all made the mistake of staying in the company area."

Henry Holt shook his head. "Welcome to your day off."

"This is fucked up. What's the point of an off-duty day if you just get roped into some shit detail?" Danny Rogers whined.

Everyone mumbled in agreement.

"You have to hide to get your day off around here," Henry added.

The Sergeant returned with a paper in his hand. "Monsoons are coming soon, and we need to build a shelter for our weapons cleaning area. Here's the diagram of what we want. Holt, I'm putting you in charge of the detail."

Henry glanced at the other men, signaling it wasn't his idea to be the fall guy. He took the Sergeant's paper and carefully examined the drawing with instructions for dimensions and post placements.

"Don't make a day of this! You should be able to complete the job in a few hours. Get shovels and anything else you need from Supply."

"Got it, Sarge," Henry replied.

"If you need anything else, come find me. I'll be in the area all day," the Sergeant ordered and promptly walked away.

"I guess he has something more important to do," Danny remarked, clearly disgusted.

"Yeah, like find patsies, ditch the work, and then cut and run," Ben snarled.

Danny turned to Henry and slapped him on the back. "We don't blame you, man. You got double-fucked. Not only do you lose a day off, but you get to be the new boss."

## Cementing Our Future

Henry pointed to a building behind the assembly area. "There's where we'll work. I have construction experience, so maybe that's why the Sarge put me in charge of the detail. Anyway, here's the basic plan. The shelter will be thirty feet by twelve feet. What we'll do first is frame an area for a concrete pad. We'll anchor four posts in the ground and cover the area with a tin roof that extends off the end of this building. Next, we'll build a work table where guys can clean weapons after they return from patrol or convoy."

"It makes sense because we need this shelter. I hate cleaning weapons in the rain," Danny stated.

"I agree, but it sucks that we have to do it on our day off. Why couldn't they have assigned it to someone else as a duty assignment?" Dave complained.

"What the fuck is your problem? We're in Vietnam, you idiot. What difference does it make? Your ass belongs to Uncle Sam every day. You telling me you got a hot date or you're planning to go for a hike?" Henry retorted.

Tension spiked, and the group fell silent.

"It's bad enough that we're on detail. Let's not make it worse by bickering with each other," Ben chimed in.

"Fuck you, Long!" Dave snapped. "You college boys think you're so smart. You probably don't even know how to lay cement."

"You're right, I've never laid cement. But at least I'm smart enough not to shit where I eat!" Ben snapped back.

"What's that supposed to mean, asshole?" Dave lunged toward Ben.

Henry grabbed him by the arm and shouted, "Everyone shut up and get your act together! We're not wasting time whining and acting like idiots. The Sarge put me in charge of this detail, and I'll be damned if I'm going to spend any more time working than is necessary. Don't you understand the only way to save part of your day is to get the damn job done as fast as we can?"

The group again fell silent, but frustration and tension filled the air.

Henry composed himself and continued, "Long and Hernandez, get a wheelbarrow and bring the cement here. Rogers and I will go to Supply and get tools and lumber to frame the pad, put up posts, and complete the roof rafters."

They all nodded and headed out as assigned. It took an hour to gather all the required materials. By the time they returned, the tension had subsided.

Henry directed the men to work as a team. They dug a trench and assembled the pad frame. They then mixed the cement and poured it into the cavity to fill and level it.

Now focused on their tasks, they worked in unison. They worked in pairs, dug four corner holes, set posts, and poured cement to anchor them. It took a couple of hours to finish that stage of the project. At 11:30, they broke for chow.

After thirty minutes, they returned to the worksite and found Sergeant Bruffer inspecting their progress.

"What do you think, Sarge?" Henry asked.

Everyone shifted uncomfortably in the heat, waiting for the Sergeant's response. Beads of sweat ran down the side of Ben's face.

"Our next step is to put up the roof framing, but this cement must set for twenty-four hours before we can put weight on those posts," Henry continued.

"You did a good job with the cement pad," the Sergeant replied. "It looks level and full to the corners. Good work, Holt."

Henry pointed to the other guys. "It was a team effort, Sarge. Everyone pulled their weight to get this done."

The Sergeant nodded, still examining the construction site.

"I know you understand the importance of curing time for cement. The worst thing we can do is put weight it on too soon. We've prepared a good foundation. We'll allow the cement to cure properly. Tomorrow we can install the roof rafters, attach the metal sheets, and finish the cleaning table."

Everyone held their breath as the Sergeant looked at Henry, then at the pad and posts. He turned toward the detail team and asserted, "You've done a good day's work. I'll tell the Captain we need to let the cement fully cure. Take the rest of the day off." The Sergeant returned to HQ.

Ben and the others breathed a sigh of relief. *That's the right decision. That's especially wise because you're going to need our support in the future, especially on the highway.*

## The Beat Goes On

They all congratulated each other, "Great work, team!"

"Let's get out of this heat," Dave suggested.

"Gather the tools and return everything to Supply," Holt directed.

"Then let's go to the Club for a cold beer," Dave added.

Danny nodded gleefully. "Great idea! It's air-conditioned."

"So is HQ, but none of us are welcome to hang out there," Ben chimed in. They all laughed and nodded in agreement.

"You guys made me look good. I'll buy the first round," Henry offered.

After returning everything to Supply, they gathered at the EM Club.

"We did a good job for a bunch of unskilled workers," Dave declared.

"That area's going to be a big hit with the guys," Danny remarked.

"Especially when it rains," Henry added. "Everyone will appreciate having some protection while cleaning weapons."

"That's for sure," Ben echoed. "I've noticed some guy's shortcut their cleaning process when it's raining. That's not good! We all know combat effectiveness and that our security depends on clean weapons."

"You're dead right on that point," Danny added. "That covered area means guys won't hurry and shortcut an important task just to get out of the rain."

A song by Sonny and Cher, "The Beat Goes On," played in the background.

Dave took another gulp. "You know, I was pissed when I got pulled for this detail, but I know everybody will appreciate this shelter. I'm proud of what we accomplished."

"You couldn't have said it better," Henry nodded and took another swig. "We're here for three sixty-five and a wake-up. We all want to be safe."

Everyone nodded, but Ben wondered, *Where's he going with this?*

"Most days, we can't see what we've accomplished, but today we can. Every day we'll look at that shelter and know we did that."

Ben echoed the song's lyrics. "And men keep marching off to war."

"Yea, as the song says, the beat goes on," Danny added. "Let's raise our glasses and drink to making sure the beat goes on for each of us."

"And let's especially raise our glasses that all who've marched off to war get home safe," Henry proposed.

"We can all drink to that, brother!" Dave declared as he raised his glass.

"Amen to that!" Ben exclaimed after a toast to a job well done.

## Letter Home 129: *April 23, 1970; 1900 hours*

*Darling Angel:*

*I love you! Would you be interested if I could buy you a piece of silk 12 feet by 3 feet for $12.00? It comes in several colors and I will buy you as much as you wish. I also can get 3 feet by 3 feet from $3.00. If you would like to make yourself some clothes from silk just let me know.*

*I sent my sister a birthday card and told her to let you read it when you visit. Please do because it is worthwhile.*

*I'm very tired because I did a lot of manual labor today. I'm working on a suntan too.*

*I'm enclosing this article because it appears to be very interesting. Comment if you wish. I made a wild discovery today – I took a close look at a couple of Johnny's pictures and they looked familiar. Ask my mother to show you my baby pictures. Our son looks exactly like me in a couple of pictures.*

*I've been working in the company area on details the last two days but I go back to work as an MP on the highway tomorrow. I got my back sunburned today while mixing and laying cement.*

*I'm happy today because I looked at my picture album (and liked very much what I saw). It is good to look at pictures of you because it makes me feel good. Please send me a new picture of you. I'd like to see how your hair is growing.*

*Your Loving Husband,*

*Ben*

# DEATH ON THE
# SHOULDER: Helpless

## April 24, 1970

### Comfortable Routine

Ben stood waiting to draw weapons from the Armory. "I'm feeling more comfortable every day."

"Yeah, me too! It's not even been a month, and I've already developed a rhythm working the highway," Tucker Bronson agreed.

"My cadence feels systematic. I don't have to concentrate going through the paces."

"Well, you better concentrate now, or you'll be late for guard mount. It's oh-six-hundred."

They hurried to the assembly area and barely joined the assembly as the Platoon Sergeant commanded, "Fall In!" He reviewed assignments and dismissed the men.

"Our vehicle's ready," Ben announced.

"Good, we have to be off-post by oh-six-forty-five," Tucker replied as he picked up the mic. "Papa Mike Oscar, this is Charlie One, radio check, over."

"Sunrise is my favorite part of the day; I never get tired of seeing that orange ball rise and light up the sky. The colors are incredible as they change."

"What the hell are you now? A poet?"

"Maybe someday! But today, I'm just happy to enjoy this beauty— nature is showing us that peace on earth is possible."

"You smoke too much dope! There'll never be peace on earth."

Ben frowned but didn't reply. *I'm not taking the bait. It's too beautiful a morning to spoil it by arguing with Tucker. He's impossible! I'm going to enjoy this drive in peace.*

He exited the main gate and drove the next twelve miles in silence.

Tucker broke the tranquility, "My favorite part of the day is this free-fire period. There are no gooks on the road between twenty hundred and oh-seven-hundred hours. This place is okay when there aren't any Vietnamese to spoil it."

Ben only half-listened. *I love to drive, no matter what the conditions. I know a lot of MPs get frustrated with the crazy Vietnamese drivers. Not me! My feeling of safety is at its peak when I'm in control of the vehicle. After driving in Chicago, I think I can handle anyplace.*

They conducted several patrol loops through their AO and visited Static Post 11 during the first hours of their shift.

*Today's been peaceful so far, and I like it.*

## Another Accident Scene

Immersed in conversation, neither paid attention to the first radio call, "Charlie One, Charlie One, this is Papa Mike Oscar."

A minute passed when the radio crackled again, "Charlie One, this is Papa Mike Oscar. Acknowledge!"

Tucker grabbed the mic and replied, "Papa Mike Oscar, this is Charlie One."

"That PMO radio operator is an arrogant smart ass FNG from

New Jersey. He hasn't worked patrol or even been off-post, but he pretends he understands everything about being on the highway," Ben complained.

"Charlie One, sorry to wake you, but you've got an accident near Sierra Papa One One. Proceed to location and secure traffic until White Mice and medical arrive," the PMO radio operator directed.

Tucker smirked and replied, "Roger, cherry, ah, Papa Mike Oscar. We're Ten One One to that One Four." He turned to Ben, "I agree! There's nothing more annoying than a new guy who pretends to be experienced."

Ben flipped the siren switch. "Here we go! Watch the right as I turn around. We don't want to be an accident on the way to an accident."

*Pulling a 180 on this highway's a dangerous move, even when traffic conditions appear safe. These drivers are unpredictable. Some hit their brakes while others speed up.*

Ben pivoted to check traffic, sharply turned the steering wheel, and punched the gas to accelerate. With the siren screaming, he weaved aggressively through traffic toward Newport Bridge. "We can get there in ten minutes at sixty miles an hour!"

They arrived at the scene, and Ben pulled onto the shoulder behind a Vietnamese truck. *I'm relieved this accident doesn't seem to be as bad as that bloody highway incident I worked on a couple of weeks ago.*

"There's only a truck here. Where the fuck's the accident?" Ben wondered aloud.

"Yeah, and look at those guys on One One. This accident's right in front of them, but they call it in instead of covering it themselves," Tucker angrily added.

Ben shook his head. *Tucker has a negative attitude about everything!*

"You know they're not allowed to move off their position."

"That's a bullshit excuse," Tucker argued. "They could have walked thirty yards to the road."

"This accident is on the opposite side of the highway. It would mean those MPs would abandon their vehicle to cross the road. That's not protocol."

"That's what causes friction between patrols and static posts. The SPs use that excuse to sit on their ass and let us do all the work. I think they resent our freedom of movement."

"Our patrol responsibilities require that we deal with road situations. Accidents are the messy part of conducting patrol."

"I hate this! Fucking gooks can't drive for shit. We should leave them out here. We can't do anything anyway. What's the point of coming to these accidents?"

Ben tried to prevent the argument from escalating. "Okay, you cover traffic, and I'll check the accident."

Tucker walked a few yards up the road and vigorously waved his nightstick at the southbound traffic, directing them to the left and around the accident.

Ben walked toward the truck but didn't see anything that warranted the call. He continued past the transport and found a mangled moped under the front bumper. *It looks like the truck hit a moped, but both these vehicles are Vietnamese. We have no jurisdiction at this accident scene.*

He looked back toward Tucker, controlling traffic in the road. *At least I'm safe here. Tucker's narrowed the southbound traffic to one lane, and vehicles are moving slow and don't pose a safety risk.*

He then spotted a middle-aged Vietnamese man lying prone on his back, mumbling in Vietnamese. *I can't give any medical assistance to this man because he's not an American. But there's no reason I can't look him over for blood or broken bones.*

He didn't notice much bleeding. *What the fuck! This guy's penis is hanging out of his pants.*

He glanced toward the slowly passing vehicles to see bus passengers gawking at the scene. *I feel bad for this guy, even if he is a gook. And these gawkers are pissing me off! Why can't people mind their own business?*

"Didi!" he shouted and waved for them to look away. *That was ridiculous! Passengers don't control a bus's speed, but they always seem to have a morbid curiosity about accidents.*

Ben looked back at the injured man. *Should I do something to protect this guy's privacy? I feel awkward, but his circumstances are embarrassing. I don't know if there's anything I can do.*

He stepped into the highway's empty right lane and looked each way. "Nothing! Where the hell are the White Mice? Damn them! They should be here dealing with this!"

## My Poncho, His Life

The injured man's speech slowed to being barely audible. His body twitched, and a strangely twisted grimace crossed his face.

*I wonder if he's cold. I remember from medical training that one thing to do is keep the victim warm. We can't administer treatment, but keeping him covered shouldn't violate protocol. We don't have blankets, but I have a poncho.*

He walked back to the vehicle next to where Tucker directed traffic. "What's happening?"

"The victim was on a moped, and he's pretty messed up. I'm getting my poncho to cover him, maybe help keep him warm."

"Don't bother, man. Vietnamese aren't our problem. Besides, you'll need your poncho when the rain comes."

"I'm not giving it away, just using it for now."

"Whatever, man. It's your shit."

Ben rummaged through his go-bag and found the heavy poncho at the bottom. He returned to the accident scene and draped it over the injured man. He no longer tried to speak or even moved.

*Where the hell are the White Mice? What's taking them so long? There are two National Police stations within five miles. One's at the Thu Duc intersection, and the other's only two miles away at Newport Docks. It shouldn't take this long to get here.*

He looked to his left and spotted the Vietnamese truck driver, squatting in the shade smoking a cigarette. He stared at Ben with no expression.

*How can a guy who just hit somebody be so indifferent? Maybe Tucker's right. These Vietnamese don't have any regard for life, so this situation means nothing to him, except there's a delay in his day.*

Ben checked his watch. *Damn, it feels like I've been on the scene a long time, but only fifteen minutes have passed.*

He heard police sirens in the distance. *Finally! It's about fucking time the White Mice got here. I hope they're not as indifferent as this truck driver, but I'm not too confident based on what I've seen so far.*

He heard a groan, followed by a hiss that sounded like air released from a balloon. He looked closely at the man's face. *I'm not sure, but I think this guy just died.* He leaned down to see if the man was breathing. After a minute of no movement from his chest, Ben gently pulled the poncho over the man's face.

## Last Image

The White Mice finally arrived and pulled to the shoulder in front of the Vietnamese truck. They casually climbed out and motioned traffic to move faster. None of them came to where the man laid. They acted as if their only responsibility was to control traffic.

*Their actions are consistent with what I've seen over here. White Mice have an exaggerated sense of their importance and like to flaunt their authority. They deserve their reputation for being abusive toward civilians.*

Tucker walked over to Ben, "What happened to the guy?"

"Not sure what happened, but I don't think he made it."

"Damn these people!" Tucker snapped. "They drive like idiots and cause senseless accidents. I hate providing security at these scenes. This assignment is a total waste of our time!"

Ben felt numb as he stared at the bulge under his poncho.

"Well, are you or not?" Tucker raised his voice. "Long, are you listening?"

"What?"

"I asked are you going to take your poncho?"

"I can't erase the image of that guy staring at me and then dying. I was the last thing he saw," Ben mumbled.

"He's a fucking gook, for Christ's sake. Who gives a shit?"

Tucker's voice faded into the background, blending with the drone of traffic noise. Dazed and in a fog, Ben drifted off again. *I'm overwhelmed by this stranger's death and what it means to me. I'm in Vietnam, trying to avoid death and pretending that death won't touch me. Sometimes I imagine I'm already dead so I can push away my fears about dying. But today, death forced itself on me. I feel exposed and vulnerable, stripped of any illusion. I've lost my shield.*

"Damn! When the hell are we leaving?" Tucker demanded.

Ben continued to stare at the lifeless form under his poncho.

"Long! Damn it, grab your fucking poncho and let's get out of here!" Tucker shouted as he tugged on Ben's sleeve.

Ben felt the pull and mechanically replied, almost in a whisper, "Leave it. I will leave it. It's his poncho now."

"Whatever! Let's get the fuck out of here," Tucker pleaded as he continued to tug on Ben's sleeve. "Our work's done here. We've got to get back on patrol."

The White Mice still hadn't checked the victim.

*They act like he doesn't exist or that he doesn't matter.*

The Vietnamese truck driver still squatted under his vehicle, casually smoking his cigarette.

*That guy acts like he's on a work break!*

Ben moved listlessly behind Tucker toward the vehicle. "This place is fucked up. We gotta get out of here, or we'll all go crazy and become as numb as those bastards."

"Looks like it might be too late for that, at least for you."

They returned to the jeep and radioed the PMO that the National Police had secured the scene. Ben swung out into traffic, nearly colliding with another Vietnamese truck. He cruised north, but his mind remained at the location of the injured man's death. *Did he have a family? Will they know what happened? An ambulance will take his body to the morgue, but what if no one can identify him? His family may never see him again. His life, last seen, is lost forever.*

He worried about the implications of his own death. *What if I were lost in the jungle or the river with no way to recover my body? That would have a terrible impact on those who need to mourn my loss.*

Ben spotted another roadside shrine on the shoulder. *I don't understand all Vietnamese beliefs, but I think they place those little boxes along the road as some ancestral remembrance. But if the family never hears about this accident, there'll be no consecration for him, and his family won't have the opportunity to honor him properly. They'll believe his spirit will wander for all time. I hope he felt some comfort that I treated him with compassion. At least I was kinder than Tucker's disdain or the White Mice's indifference. I know if I were dying, I'd hope there would be someone who took mercy on me in my last moments of life.*

"You were stupid to leave your poncho," Tucker insisted.

"No, it had death on it. That's not good for me," Ben countered.

"Well, I guess you're right."

Ben continued to drive but with an otherworldly sense of his surroundings. *What a tragedy! My poncho is the least I could give to a dying man. More was needed, and maybe more should have been done, but our rules dictate we not provide Vietnamese medical assistance. All we can do is helplessly watch as death takes them. I'm afraid those images from the roadside will never be forgotten.*

# DREAD: Twilight Zone of Horror

## April 24, 1970

### Depressing Effect

Randy DeMarco entered the hooch and spotted his friend Ben sitting on his bunk. "What's got you down, man?"

Ben looked up but didn't respond.

"I saw what happened,," Randy added. "It was that accident, wasn't it?"

"You mean that snafu near the Newport Bridge?"

"Yeah, I was on SP-11, remember? We called it into the PMO."

"Guess I forgot it was you."

"Hell of a situation. Tucker says you went off the deep end."

"Fuck Tucker. He doesn't give a shit about anything except himself."

"He acts that way, but I'm asking about you, not Tucker."

"How I'm doing? Frustrated, pissed off, and depressed. How's that for starters?"

Randy sat on the next bunk and studied Ben's face.

"You were there and saw everything. Nobody gives a shit about anything. Tucker's an ass, but the truck driver and the White Mice belong in that cesspool of inhumanity too!" Ben ranted.

Randy nodded but said nothing.

"They send us to these accidents and then tie our hands. All we can do is direct traffic and watch human misery. I hate it!"

"It's a helpless situation," Randy sighed.

"It's fucked up and sickening. We stand by helplessly at horrific scenes. It's too much."

"You want to help, but you can't."

"And people who can do something, like the White Mice, act like their only priority is to keep vehicles moving. They're worse than useless. It's immoral."

"It doesn't make sense."

"I dread going to these accidents. It's depressing."

"I agree. We go, and then we're restrained from helping people. That's contrary to my sense of decency, too."

## Becoming Numb

Ben shifted and stared off into space. "There's horror at these accidents, and it's not limited to the victims. I think the White Mice's behavior is uglier than the physical injuries to the people."

"A lot of us see it the same way."

Ben set his gaze on Randy like a laser beam. "How do you cope with these situations?"

Randy paused and shook his head. "All I can do is pray for the victims. Sometimes I even pray for the White Mice. Maybe their compassion has died. Maybe they've seen so much they've become numb to the misery."

"I can't keep doing this. I get angrier with each accident, and I want to rip into the White Mice. I feel I should administer medical assistance, but I know I'll get in trouble for violating protocol."

"I understand your frustration, but that will only make things worse."

Ben sighed heavily. "Then my only alternative is to detach. I'll have to become as indifferent as the White Mice and that asshole Tucker."

"That's a terrible option. You would have to stop caring about people because you care so much."

"I don't know what else to do! These accident scenes are emotional torture. I need a way to shield myself, or these situations are going to tear me apart. If I don't find a way to deal with it, I might end up hurting myself too."

"I get it. A lot of guys struggle with that dilemma."

"Maybe I should adopt Tucker's attitude that they mean nothing."

"Do you believe that?"

Ben hung his head and stammered, "No, but the conflict is ripping me apart. Human decency is important, but if I'm doing nothing, what's that say about me?"

Randy placed his hand on Ben's shoulder. "It means you're a decent human in a terrible situation with no option other than to obey orders. In these circumstances, it isn't you. It's about the contradictions and moral challenges."

"These situations are a direct assault on my moral compass."

"Sometimes there are circumstances when all we can do is accept the conditions that we don't control. Try to remember how important it is to trust in the Lord and have faith that things happen for a reason."

"I'm having a hard time seeing the reason for what's happening."

"I don't mean reason from a rational and logical perspective. Things happen in life, and sometimes they're terrible. We have to believe that something good can come from bad circumstances. That's why I say things happen for a reason. Powerful lessons and personal strength can result from terrible experiences," Randy explained.

## No Exit, No Peace

"I hope that happens; at least that means something good can come out of it. It feels like we're in hell, facing moral and emotional trauma every time we're at an accident. It reminds me of a *Twilight Zone* episode where a guy is trapped in a terrifying environment with no way to get out. There's no exit from a nightmare that never ends."

"That's an interesting metaphor. Vietnam's a hall of mirrors, and we can't find an exit. But what's worse is the images are distorted moral characterizations of ourselves. That's a nightmare of unbearable mental anguish."

Ben's replied in a barely audible voice, "Well, if these experiences are happening for a reason, and our challenge is to learn, I want to say I hate this school. I prefer a less tortured way to learn the lessons."

"Sometimes people learn their greatest lessons from the school of hard knocks."

"I feel like I'll go crazy before I graduate."

"No one promised life would be easy. Lots of people go through much harder experiences. Rape, murder, child abuse, poverty, disease—"

"So quit complaining? Vietnam isn't the worst school?" Ben interrupted.

"No, just saying people endure lots of tough conditions. These happen to be the ones we face."

"Okay. Point made."

"Remember, we're told in First Corinthians 10 that the Lord won't let us be tempted beyond our strength. He won't give us more than we can handle."

"So becoming numb isn't my only option."

"You're getting my point."

"There's still no peace in this situation."

"Peace happens in the afterlife, Ben. Today you're in Vietnam."

Ben threw up his hands. "Don't remind me! I was trying to forget."

"Fat chance of that happening!"

## The Images I Can't Erase

Ben stared at the floor and confessed, "Speaking of things we're trying to forget, that image is seared into my mind."

"What image?"

"The face of the man on the shoulder of the highway."

"Maybe that's a good thing?"

"Good thing? How does the face of a dying man become a good thing?"

Randy pondered the question, studying Ben's tortured expression. "It sounds like he was going to die no matter what you could have done for him. It's not about the man dying – it's about your compassion for him. That's the positive side that you should hold tightly. That's your compassion fighting against an inhuman circumstance. Hold onto that as you seek meaning from the promise in Romans 8: in everything the Lord works out his goodwill according to his purpose."

"But the image haunts me," Ben protested. "It's disturbing to remember."

"That's good. It means your conscious is alive and fighting for you."

Ben stared at Randy with no response.

"I sense you're not sure about that?"

"It's not the way I've thought about those images."

"Maybe it's a better way to think about all of this. Maybe your feelings of dread and depression are just a negative perspective, kind of like Tucker's attitude. They don't mean nothing," Randy suggested.

Ben continued to think about the implications in silence.

"There's another perspective to consider, Ben. Try to interpret these experiences as an invitation to reaffirm your character and convictions. Reflect on your inner self as a source of strength that can provide wisdom from a direction you never expected."

Ben leaned on his bunk and stared at the men playing cards. "Maybe I could try that. That's a different lens, for sure. I sure don't have anything to lose."

## Letter Home 130: *April 27, 1970; 0800 hours*

*My Darling Angel:*

*I love you! I'm finally at the dentist's office. By now it feels like I have about four abscessed teeth and the rest are rotten. I guess Vietnam is not the place to raise a healthy kid. I have an appointment with the eye doctor for May 2.*

*Did I tell you that my extension was approved? I ETS January 20, 1971.*

*Just think, 1970 will have never existed in my life!*

*Did you ever get the Easter flowers? You never mentioned them so I guess they didn't get there. I was going to send some for Mother's Day (remember you are one now) but there is no sense if they won't get there.*

*I'll send you 10 cards instead. I love you so much my darling.*

*It was a strange coincidence to receive your letter about the funeral home visit when I did. I had covered an accident that afternoon and it was the first time a person had died on me. Normally, either there are slight injuries or else the people are immediately dead. This person was quite alive when I got there but I don't know what happened.*

*He was just lying there waiting for the ambulance and I knelt down and said "it will be here soon." Then I stood up and said something to another MP. When I turned around he had the blank stare and somebody checked his pupils and pulse. Dead.*

*It was very original experience and I didn't really react because I was so surprised.*

*I will probably see plenty more before I leave here but I doubt that I'll mention them again in letters. We have more important things to talk about.*

*As far as R & R goes – we could get a place to stay after we get to Hawaii. That is normal for R & R since most GIs don't get a chance to* make reservations. I do not feel that I have enough information available to make a choice and do not have time to find it (I can barely find time to write you every two or three days).

If you feel that you know what's happening and want to, then please do make any reservations you can. However, I do not know for sure if I can go in June and will not find out for another three to five weeks. I'll let you know for sure as soon as I'm told.

You also mentioned some army place for R & R. I really don't care to spend my R & R from Vietnam on an army post.

But I'll leave it up to you – 8 months and 23 days to go.

Personally, I hate the army, and if I was not so close (ha ha) to ETS (end tour of service) I would go crazy. I hope time goes as fast in the next 8-plus months as it has the last one.

P.S. I love you. I may not get to call before R & R. Be happy I could the first 4 months instead of sad I could not the last 10. It could have been 14.

All my love forever,

Ben

# RESENTMENT:
# American Woman

## April 27, 1970

### Dental Appointment

Ben methodically buttoned his fatigues and laced his jungle boots. *After sixteen months in the Army, they've finally scheduled me to have my teeth checked. It doesn't make sense that they ordered me to report for a dental inspection but still require me to report as a sick call. I'm not ill, just following orders. Like most practices, the Army way isn't necessarily the logical way.*

"Long reporting for sick call," Ben announced upon entering HQ.

The clerk looked up from his paperwork and replied, "Roger that."

The Staff Sergeant on duty was an old Army dog. He had been too long in the service and responded cynically to everything. "What's your sissy excuse, soldier? Tummy ache from too much drinking? Maybe homesick and missing your mama?"

Ben bit his tongue. *I'm not going to tangle with this old fart; besides, he's tired and irritable from being on duty all night. He knows a soldier is required to immediately report for sick call instead of waiting for guard mount. That extra time is needed to adjust the duty roster so that Sergeants can cancel days off and reassign those men for duty.*

"No, Sergeant. I didn't drink, and I don't miss mama one damn bit. I have orders to report to the dentist."

"Damn pampered soldiers today. You kids can't handle anything. When I was your age, I was so busy killing Nazis that I didn't brush my teeth for three months."

"Yes, Sergeant. I expect you killed them all. That's why we have the luxury of going to the dentist."

"This Army has gotten too soft. Maybe it's from coddling you spoiled brats. We've dropped our standards too low by bringing all you shiftless draftees into our fine institution!" the Sergeant shouted.

Ben glanced sideways toward the clerk, also a draftee. He turned away and focused on paperwork to stay clear of the Sergeant's tirade.

*That old buzzard sure is worked up about something. Who knows, maybe this intergenerational tension has been boiling all night.*

"I'm sick of dealing with you people," the Sergeant continued.

*I'll bet he's a mean bastard back home with his kids. I'm not going to get into a fight with this old NCO.*

"Yes, Sergeant. If you want me to skip the dentist and report for duty, just give the order. I'm here to follow orders and will follow yours," Ben offered, hoping to lessen the tension and disengage from an argument he couldn't win.

"You're a smart-ass, Long. Don't provoke me. You know damn well you're required to report for sick call for a dentist appointment."

*I hate these antagonistic assholes. That's my point, so just shut the fuck up! I learned at home that I can't reason with a close-minded person.* "Yes, Sergeant."

"All right, you reported, now get the hell out of here. We've got more important things to handle, and you're wasting our time!" the Sergeant barked.

Ben nodded and quickly exited the HQ, relieved to escape that tirade. He walked toward the mess hall and ran into Tucker Bronson on his way to guard mount.

"Why aren't you going out? You on sick call?" Tucker asked.

"Dentist," Ben replied in a curt tone, expecting to hear more crap.

"Good for you. I wish I could get one of those appointments. Sure beats spending the day in the sun."

Ben finished a flavorless breakfast and returned to the barracks. Thirty minutes later, Tucker entered the hooch with Bruce Bugliano. "Hey, Long, we're your ride to the dentist. Get your ass moving."

Ben hurried out with them and jumped into the jeep. He was confused when the patrol vehicle headed toward the main gate. "Where the hell are you taking me? Bien Hoa?"

"No. The Army dentist is near the 90th Replacement Compound. It's faster to go around the perimeter; otherwise, we do a slow crawl across the base," Tucker explained.

They arrived at the base's other gate in five minutes and drove a short distance to a two-story building marked Medical Services.

"Say hi to the dental assistant," Bruce smirked. "She's the sister of Mia Wa, my girlfriend from the 90th Replacement PX."

"We'll return in ninety minutes to take you back to the company area," Tucker explained.

Usually, a dentist's visit wouldn't be enjoyable, but that office was air-conditioned and furnished with comfortable chairs. The exam was painless, and the dentist polite and considerate. *This place is fancy. Evidently, the standard-issue isn't standard everywhere. Some in the Army have it a lot better than others, I guess. And the visit's a lot nicer than my experiences as a kid. Those were frightening! I wonder if the dentist feels guilty that he's working in an air-conditioned environment knowing his patients spend their days in the heat and humidity.*

Ben snuck sideways glances at the dental assistant, a young and petite female. *I'll bet having a pretty Vietnamese assistant is a pleasant benefit. She must be Tam, Mia Wa's older sister. She's stunning!*

*I'd volunteer to go to the dentist every day to see her. I wouldn't be surprised if there's a romantic relationship between these two. Any guy would flip over her, and dentists get lonely too.*

## Hooch Maid Kim

Ben's time in the dentist's office passed too quickly.

Tucker and Bruce arrived on time. "So, what did you think about Tam?" Bruce asked.

"She's stunning."

"Isn't she? I still think Mia Wa's the girl for me. She may not be as pretty, but she's friendlier. Beautiful girls tend to be aloof and arrogant."

"When a girl looks that good, she can afford to be conceited."

"There's a lot of truth to that. It's like that Jimmy Soul song says If you want to be happy for the rest of your life."

"Enough talk about your moonstruck romance," Tucker interrupted. "We'd better get moving; otherwise, we'll be singing a different song, called, *if you want to continue to work on patrol. . .*"

"Okay, fine," Bruce acknowledged. "Let's get Ben back, and we'll return to patrolling the highway."

They dropped Ben in the company area just before 10:00 a.m., and he went to HQ to report. He was grateful the ornery Sergeant was gone. *Hope that old man gets some sleep and wakes up in a better mood,* he mused as he headed toward the barracks.

He glanced at the weapons cleaning shelter and paused to admire the new structure. *That looks good. It was a pain to get roped into working on a day off, but we'll all appreciate having a covered work area when the monsoons come. I hope I don't get snatched for another work detail today, though.*

The barracks for the day patrol platoon was empty, except for a couple of guys on sick call or assigned a day off. Ben pulled his writing pad from the footlocker and turned on his radio to Armed Forces Radio. *Music helps me relax, and when I close my eyes, I can picture myself back in the world.*

He settled back to start a letter when he spotted Kim, a twenty-something Vietnamese girl, enter the barracks and begin to slowly sweep the floor. *Those hooch maids are in our unit every day. Their presence has become so routine they're practically invisible as they do their housekeeping and laundry duties.*

Kim worked her way down the aisle and asked, "Laundry? Shine?"

Deep in thought, Ben didn't notice Kim's approach. "I'm good."

"MP Numba one!" Kim echoed and repeated, "Laundry? Shine?"

*I guess she misunderstands the phrase. When I say I'm good, it means no thanks.* "No laundry, no shine," Ben replied.

Kim moved to the next man and asked the same questions, and Ben watched the guy flirt with the girl. *He's lonely! Some guys would like to get a little of that hooch maid, but engaging in sexual relations is strictly forbidden. On the other hand, who knows what happens in the senior NCOs' private quarters. We all wonder while rumors fly! That's so typical in an all-male culture, especially since sex is our favorite fantasy.*

Ben watched as Kim sashayed down the aisle. *She knows what she's doing, and it doesn't help that these hooch girls don't wear bras. Except for those other two guys, we're the only people here. Hopefully, it'll be quiet enough for me to concentrate on writing.*

## Resentment

Ben returned to his letter, half-listening to music when he was startled by Kim's voice, "American woman number ten."

He looked up to find her glaring at him. He looked at the picture of Sue displayed in his footlocker and then back at her. *Is she upset that I'm writing a letter home?*

"American woman number ten," Kim repeated, clearly angry. She stopped sweeping and pointed her broom handle toward the radio.

"American woman, gonna mess your mind. Say A, say M, say E, say R, say I, and C, say A, N. American woman, gonna mess your mind," the singer crooned the familiar lyrics by the song from The Guess Who.

"American woman number ten. Vietnamese number one," Kim added.

"American woman, get away from me. American woman, mama, let me be," the refrain continued.

Kim was visibly upset. Ben tried to make sense of it, but he was stunned. *This situation is crazy; those lyrics aren't a love song praising American women. They're a cynical rejection of American culture.*

Kim continued to glare at him and waited. When Ben didn't respond, she grew even more agitated. She threw her straw broom to the floor and stomped away.

Dumbfounded and baffled, Ben watched her storm out of the hooch while the song continued to play. *What the fuck was that about?*

Kim's outburst lasted only two minutes, but it stung like a firefight—briefly intense followed by an eerie silence. *Why did she react like that? Why is she so upset about "American Woman"? She doesn't understand the lyrics; otherwise, I'd expect her to agree with the message. Her outburst doesn't make sense unless this is a sexual thing.*

## Clashes

He tried to return to his writing, but the image of Kim's rage replayed in his mind. *I'm not sure what to think. What are the attitudes or emotions of the Vietnamese women that work for us? Have they developed personal connections with us? Was her emotional outburst because of jealousy?*

Ben recalled other interactions with Vietnamese that resulted in clashes, especially recent frictions with ARVN QCs (Army of the Republic of Vietnam, South Vietnam, Military Police). *And what about other relationships? I'll never forget the squabble at Saigon Port's Gate 7. One of the White Mice asked me to buy a Playboy magazine from the PX and then was offended when I refused. Have Vietnamese policemen developed close relations with other MPs, so he felt betrayed by me? Maybe he expected all Americans to show the same kind of cooperation. It sure seemed like he expected me to buy the magazine. He assumed he could ask, and I would agree.* (See 2nd Moon: Temptation, Story 24 ~ Power and Privilege).

*Is there a fundamental problem of misjudging one another's intention? We tend to tread carefully in these partnerships. We pretend we're friends, but our interactions are guarded and superficial. Maybe there's a deeper problem than we realize between our cultures. If the Vietnamese expect Americans to behave like we're friends, that will cause conflict when MPs act aloof or even hostile. Maybe the chasm we're struggling across is more than cultural. How much of this problem is an attitude of racism? The Army drilled into our heads that Vietnamese are gooks, the enemy, and less advanced than us. After that indoctrination, why would GIs be willing to form personal relationships?*

Ben stared at his unfinished letter then laid down his pen. He stared at the floor, shaking his head. *I'm not going to mention this encounter with Kim. It's complicated enough trying to manage our relationship with the Vietnamese. How can I clearly explain my confusing emotions in a letter? Sue might worry that hooch maids are sex partners rather than housekeepers. I'm always talking about how horny I am here and complimenting the Vietnamese women's delicate beauty. "American Woman," you've opened an ugly can of worms this morning.*

# TEMPTATIONS:
## French Quarter

### April 28, 1970

**Dirty Laundry**

Ben partnered with Henry Holt on Charlie One patrol as the driver. Their AO bracketed Thu Duc and included key government properties, a water filtration plant, and a National Police compound. Police patrols typically doubled in that sector for enhanced security.

Henry pointed toward a distinctive residential enclave west of the highway. "Let's turn in there."

"Isn't that the French Quarter?"

"Yes, it's unique and worth exploring. The French Quarter is an exclusive zone of French colonial villas, each an acre, protected by ten-foot walls.

"Isn't this outside our authorized area?"

"You've never ventured off the highway? That's not what I heard about you."

*I guess my explorations aren't a secret. And Henry certainly knows his way around since he's been in-country several months longer than I have.*

"No, I'm good. I just wanted to be sure you knew," Ben stammered.

"Don't be a smart-ass! I know more than you'd ever suspect. Take that cut." He pointed to a lane through an opening in the wall.

"Okay, fine," Ben apologized and steered onto the shoulder.

"I need to check on something. There's nothing to worry about. We'll be back on the highway before anyone's the wiser."

Ben wheeled the jeep onto a dirt lane and rolled through the opening.

"Go past two cross lanes, then turn right," Henry instructed.

*These are thickly wooded villas. I can't see anything except concrete walls topped with shards of broken glass.*

Henry pointed to a compound with a blue steel gate. "Pull up over there. I'll ring the doorbell with three longs and one short to let them know we're safe visitors."

A large Chinese man with a pistol tucked in his waistband swung the massive gate open enough to peer out. He nodded at Henry and opened the gate barely enough to allow the jeep to enter the compound. He closed and bolted the gate behind them.

"We'll only be here a few minutes. I've got to pick up something," Henry explained as he climbed out of the jeep.

They stepped inside the villa, and cold air splashed over Ben's face. *Oh, that air-conditioning feels good. This is a fancy house; I'm in a vestibule.*

Henry continued into the parlor room, and a middle-aged Chinese woman stepped forward and greeted him. They disappeared into another room behind a beaded curtain.

*Maybe she's the matron of this place.*

Ben cautiously stepped into the parlor, momentarily blinded by sunlight reflecting off the white tile floor. He noticed three ornately trimmed windows in the ceiling. *This place reminds me of movies about colonial days. I feel like I've stepped onto a Hollywood set.*

Two large security men examined him suspiciously, and Ben stopped and stood uncomfortably. *Whoa! There's armed security inside, too. They have pistols in their waistbands. Must be some serious business going on here. They look Chinese, not Vietnamese. They're sizing me up, probably thinking the same thing I am. If there's trouble, can I handle these guys?*

He heard an animated conversation from the other room. *That sounds like Henry's voice, and maybe the woman who met us at the door?*

An uneasy few minutes passed in silence. Ben stood motionless, never taking his eyes off the security men.

Henry emerged from the back room. "The battalion has a laundry service here in the French Quarter. They clean and starch our uniforms."

"Okay," Ben replied, unsure what else to say.

"Today's a quick in-and-out visit. We don't have time to get laid or high."

*Laid or high? I thought Holt said this was a laundry business? Now I'm even more uncomfortable being here.*

"The laundry is a front for a drug distribution operation, and they have the best dope. But we're not taking unnecessary risks, at least not today. I've got several other pickups to make," Henry explained.

"So, what are we doing here?"

"Everything in the French Quarter is connected, and we can get anything we want right here. Kind of like Alice's Restaurant, if you know what I mean."

*Alice's Restaurant? Does he mean the song by Arlo Guthrie? What the hell does he mean by that?*

"You said this is the laundry service for our battalion. Are you saying these people run drugs on the side? That's pretty bold, isn't it?"

Henry's grin turned into a scowl. "This is how they like to do business. They use legitimate business fronts as a cover for illegal operations. It's safer that way. Circumstances aren't always what they appear to be."

Ben frowned but didn't respond.

"Okay, too cryptic? Let me make this real simple, Long. We're on duty, and it's illegal as hell for us to be in a whorehouse or drug den. So mums the word!"

Ben shrugged and replied, "Okay, I know that's true. I'm cool."

The matron returned and handed a package to Henry.

*Now what? That's a carton of cigarettes neatly sealed in cellophane.*

"We came here for cigarettes?" Ben asked.

"Look at the label."

"I don't know that brand, what's it say, Park Lane?"

"But they look normal enough, right?"

Ben examined the wrapping. "I don't see anything unusual, except that I've never heard of this brand."

"Exactly my point. That's the clever part! Things aren't always what they seem."

"You've lost me," Ben mumbled.

"Take a closer look at the labeling and wrapper folds. The packaging is a high-quality job. These aren't regular smokes, but they'll fool anyone conducting a search unless the guy knows the inside dope."

"Well, you've fooled me. What's the point?"

"This is a special product that's not available on the street. These are high-potency marijuana joints laced with opium. Smoke one of these and your head will spin in circles for hours. Inspect the pack again."

"This wrapping is convincing. It looks like a regular pack of cigarettes. I'd never suspect these are drugs," Ben acknowledged.

"That's why we deal with these people. They're real professionals."

Ben handed the pack back and glanced at the smiling matron.

Henry waved away the exchange. "That pack's for you, but be careful when you smoke them. They'll send you on a deep-space trip."

Ben shoved the pack into his thigh pocket. "Thanks."

"Now, let's get back on the road before someone realizes we're missing," Henry directed and moved toward the door.

## Living Two Lives

As they exited the compound gate, the radio crackled, "Papa Mike Oscar to Charlie One."

"Good timing," Henry whispered and grabbed the mic.

The PMO radio operator continued, "Charlie One, what's your ten-twenty?"

"We're approaching the Thu Duc intersection."

"Roger that," the PMO radio operator replied. "You're needed to back up Bravo One on a drug arrest near Sierra Papa One Four. Can you support?"

"Roger," Henry affirmed. "Long, mau-len! Bravo One needs help with a drug bust."

Ben pulled north onto the highway and flipped on the siren.

"Seems weird. I mean, given where we were and what we're going to do?"

"Don't confuse our job and personal lives. The job is to catch criminals and maintain law and order. But we have the right to enjoy ourselves and take pleasures that come our way."

"You mean like today?"

Henry nodded, "Sometimes we make our own opportunities. Our MP role gives us access to places that regular guys aren't allowed to visit."

*That's the paradox I've learned about police and criminal activity.*

"So we enforce the law, but we do what we want?"

Henry scowled and warned, "Don't get self-righteous, Long! We do what we have to do to get by here, but that doesn't mean we ignore opportunities to meet our personal interests. Everyone grabs the good stuff when they think they can get away with it."

Ben drove in silence.

"Hell, you're no saint, Long! I heard you had your fingers in the cookie jar in Saigon. And I know you smoke dope."

"I'm not saying I'm innocent, but isn't it ironic that we were in a whorehouse to pick up drugs when we got the call to help with a drug bust?"

Henry snapped again, "That's reality! We live two lives. Don't let contradictory circumstances mess with your mind. Keep those two worlds separate and stay focused on what's in front of you."

"But—"

"No buts," Henry interrupted. "Don't overthink this shit, man. Conflicting situations happen when you live two lives. Don't try to make sense of everything, or it'll drive you crazy. Compartmentalization – that's the trick to staying sane."

"Yeah, and make sure the next drug bust isn't me," Ben sighed as he pulled alongside patrol Bravo One at the scene.

## Economy of Crime

After evening chow, Ben hurried to the EM Club to join friends Greg Pulaski and Tucker Bronson.

"How'd it go with Holt today?" Greg asked between gulps of beer.

"I've heard he's quite a character with some impressive connections," Tucker said.

Ben shook his head. "He's something else, that's for sure."

"So, what'd you find out?" Tucker pressed.

"We went into the French Quarter."

"What'd you see?" Greg asked.

"Holt told me the enclave is an exclusive zone for French expatriates and their business partners. It's a haven for prostitution, drugs, and black-market activity."

"I've heard their clientele includes the highest echelon of Vietnamese military officers, government officials, and businessmen," Tucker interjected.

"And that there's a pretense that the French Quarter's crime-free because of the heavy presence of National Police patrols, but, in reality, the White Mice have provided a protective cocoon for the villas," Greg explained.

"There are rumors some high-ranking police officials benefit through discounted services for giving them protection," Tucker added.

"Some MPs who've worked the Combined Police Patrol (CPP) unit say the French Quarter is teeming with criminal activity. Some guys have used insider knowledge to take advantage of the opportunities for their personal benefit," Greg continued.

"No kidding! Anybody we might know?" Tucker joked with a wink.

"I couldn't say," Ben dryly replied.

"We shouldn't be surprised; there's criminal enterprise at every level of this society," Greg declared.

"But it's not necessarily because they're bad people! Theft, corruption, prostitution, drugs, and the black market are the only ways to make money in this war-torn economy. Vietnamese who aren't in the rice economy need an income, too," Ben argued.

"Gee, look who's going soft on the gooks," Tucker sniped.

"That's true. Criminal enterprise is so rampant that its economic impact is greater than the agricultural sector," Greg noted.

"Yeah, and those activities are predominately around American bases where troops drive volume. GIs fuel the black market by selling PX items for quick cash or barter for sex. You know that, and we've all been part of the problem," Ben sighed.

"I've developed a good insight into the criminal world," Greg asserted.

"I'd say we're experts! We understand it from the inside out," Tucker laughed.

"Some of us are even card-carrying members," Greg chuckled.

## Criminal Mindset

"We could have a field day if we wanted!" Ben suggested.

"What do you mean?" Tucker asked.

"I mean, think about it! The ability to identify and apprehend law-breakers is more effective when police have practical knowledge of criminal patterns. If a cop understands how criminals operate, he'd have a valuable skill for anticipating criminal behavior."

Greg nodded thoughtfully. "We *do* have practical knowledge in that area."

"You bet we do! Experienced police understand that developing a keen insight into the criminal mind is their most useful tool. Ironically, that kind of insight is best gained through directly interacting with criminals," Ben continued.

Greg smirked, "And a reliable source for insight is a personal experience in criminal activity. That insight will give you a second sense."

Tucker's face lit up, "It takes one to know one!"

"Exactly! The relationship between police and criminals is symbiotic. Without criminals, there'd be no need for cops. And although laws regulate the boundaries of acceptable social behavior, those laws also draw criminals toward opportunities," Greg affirmed.

"If CID knew we were so smart, they'd be kicking in our door – to recruit us!" Ben exclaimed.

"Well, your black market experience sure provided insight. I bet you got a real education on that world," Tucker chimed in.

"Don't forget my underage drinking and drug experiences! I might not have done well in engineering classes, but college broadened my education on how a criminal thinks," Ben crowed.

"I believe that, Kilo," Greg laughed.

"Think about it. There are advantages a guy gains by living in two worlds. Police work and criminal activity teach complementary lessons. Experience in one builds your understanding of the other," Ben posed.

"I dig it, man!" Tucker exclaimed as he gulped his beer. "We're probably the smartest MPs in the unit."

"If only they knew!" Greg agreed.

"If only," Ben echoed as he finished his beer.

*What was the Army's rationale for assigning me to the Military Police? Was this really a random assignment, or maybe they knew my background? Either way, I'm sure in an unusual situation! It reminds me of Joni Mitchell's song "Both Sides Now" because we can see this world from each perspective.*

*French Quarter villa*

# HUMPTY DUMPTY:
## A Great Fall

### April 29, 1970

**Making Adjustments**

Ben, Bruce Bugliano, and Greg Pulaski huddled in the mess hall, hurrying through breakfast before reporting to guard mount.

"I think the friction in our platoon is finally settling down," Ben remarked between bites of a bland serving of shit-on-a-shingle.

"Some guys have had a rougher time of it than others," Greg noted.

"You mean guys like Bruce and Tucker who resist Sergeant Simon's tight control methods?"

"Simon's a hard-ass. He demands we live up to his expectations and then doesn't hesitate to enforce his rules," Bruce complained, pushing away his tray.

"Sergeant Simon made his requirements very clear. Guys need to accept his expectations and make the necessary adjustments. The best way to get along with him is total compliance," Ben retorted.

"So says the suck-up!" Bruce snapped.

"Once men toe the line, he eases up on the pressure," Greg added.

"That makes Simon better than Bruffer at least," Bruce acknowledged.

"But Simon won't tolerate guys with a negative attitude," Ben posed.

"Simon gets mean with men who resist his requirements," Greg continued.

"Battles of will tend to agitate every Sergeant," Ben warned. "That's like kicking at a mean dog. They try even harder to bite you."

"I enjoy pushing back during guard mount," Bruce proudly declared.

"You're too antagonistic," Ben cautioned.

"And there are swift consequences. Guys who resist the Sergeant will feel the toe of his boot. First, he gives a kick in the ass, usually at guard mount," Greg added.

"That makes him the same as that asshole Bruffer," Bruce replied.

"His public dressing down has a purpose – to ensure the entire unit understands there will be prompt punishment for non-compliance," Ben explained.

"Oh, now you're his defender? It figures."

"Let sleeping dogs lie, Bruce," Greg interrupted. "Things could get worse. Simon will deliver other consequences."

"Yeah? Like what?"

"He'll assign you to static posts every day," Ben posed.

"If you fight him, he'll harass you non-stop to pressure you. He'll double down on breaking your spirit," Greg continued.

Ben shook his head and warned, "That's not a fight you want."

"I can handle it!" Bruce stubbornly insisted.

"But why bother? That fight isn't worth it! Just go along to get along," Ben suggested.

"Simon's constant badgering is effective, at least on the surface. Guys eventually comply with his expectations," Greg observed.

"So give to Caesar what is Caesars? Is that your advice?"

"It's the Army, man. You can't fight it forever," Ben pressed.

"Well, I got news for the Army. That battle just moves underground and fuels a counterculture. Guys who feel harassed become hostile, even if it looks like they're complying," Bruce warned.

## Loosening the Reins

"You know, there's an easier way to live. Sidestep the head-on collision and avoid all that misery," Ben advised.

"Give it some thought, man," Greg echoed. "The guys who adjust and meet Simon's expectations get positive results. The Sergeant will relax and lay off the pressure."

"That's true! Guys have been saying Simon's actually a nice guy. Acting like a badass was just a disguise to establish control. He wears disguises, too, as we talked about a couple of weeks ago," Ben added.

"You expect me to buy that shit?" Bruce challenged and stood to leave.

"It's the job, man. Leaders have to behave per Army expectations, just like we act like hard-ass MPs while on duty. Every guy's still an individual with his own personality and unique quirks," Greg explained.

"Like you, Bruce! A badass MP on the highway but a kinda decent person at the EM Club," Ben teased.

"Fuck you, Long!" Bruce snapped as he punched Ben's shoulder.

"It's time," Greg announced. "Let's get to guard mount and play the game so we can have fun on the highway without being closely monitored."

"That part I like," Bruce smiled.

"See, I knew you were smarter than you looked," Ben jabbed right back.

"Your life expectancy is getting shorter with each comment," Bruce warned.

"Just having fun, the same way as you," Ben retorted.

The men moved to their patrol vehicles after being dismissed.

"Guard mount was uneventful; an excellent start to the day," Ben noted.

"Notice the lieutenant doesn't show up anymore?" Greg asked.

"Yeah, I did. What's that all about? Maybe he doesn't want to get up for our circus?" Ben replied, placing his go bag and M-16 into the jeep.

"I think LT realizes he doesn't need to keep checking on our guard mount since things are starting to work right for Simon."

"That makes sense. I see the troublemakers, even Tucker, have finally fallen in line."

Greg turned and yelled toward Bruce at the next vehicle, "You're on SP-11, and we're on Charlie One. We'll see you out there."

"We'll be there all day. Stop by any time," Bruce replied.

"Yeah, don't forget us," his partner Ted Francisco added with a smirk.

"Ted, us guys from Detroit need to stick together. Besides, I couldn't forget you – you're too beautiful," Greg teased.

"Real funny, smart-ass!" Ted barked.

"Better than being ugly, like Bugliano," Greg continued to tease.

"Let's roll," Ben advised as he noticed Sergeant Simon watching the banter from across the assembly area.

They jumped into their vehicle and hastily exited the company area. Within minutes, they were on the highway heading south toward their AO.

"Let's make a few patrol loops in case Simon conducts an early inspection. I worry he'll try to surprise SP-11. He still has his eye on Bugliano," Greg recommended.

Ben nodded. "Bruce has been pushing his luck with snippy remarks in guard mount. Even if he dislikes him, nothing good will come from showing attitude toward Simon, especially in public."

"Yeah, he needs to keep his bad attitude to himself. He's making himself a target. Simon's proven he'll hit hard against that kind of behavior."

"It doesn't pay to go up against him, that's for sure."

"A low profile is the best defense. Speaking of that, any thoughts on what we might do today, other than rolling endlessly on this road?"

"Are you interested in checking out the French Quarter near Thu Duc, once we're sure the coast is clear?"

"Maybe, but there's the Newport docks area too. Technically we wouldn't be out of the AO since it's just over the bridge. Or we could go east toward Cat Lai. I haven't been that way yet."

"Both those ideas sound good, but I was thinking about the French Quarter because I've heard stories from guys who went there."

"You been there?"

Ben hesitated, not sure if it was wise to share his experience.

"Come on, man, we're friends," Greg pressed. "We've been through enough together that you know you can trust me. I'll keep my mouth shut."

"Okay, you're right. Yes, I was there yesterday. But that was my first time, and I don't have it all figured out yet. There are some surprises we might stumble on if we're in the right place at the right time."

"Now you've got my attention! I've heard some stories, too. Word is the French Quarter has a few opportunities we would enjoy," Greg laughed.

"Maybe even better than Mama-san's parlor on Cong Ly."

"But we need to be sure our back's covered when we slip away. I don't want to push our luck."

"Let's check with SP-11. Those guys can give us cover, and I don't want them to be a thorn in our sides when we slip away," Ben suggested.

"Yeah, we can trust Bruce. I don't know Francisco that well, but I've had a good feeling about him so far."

Ben turned onto the narrow trail and pulled alongside the static post vehicle.

"How's it going?" he asked cheerfully.

"Barrel of monkeys out here," Bruce sarcastically replied. "Can't say I've ever had more fun. These observation posts are the best thing since wooden coffins. We sit here like we're dead and watch the world go by."

"Maybe if you'd quit being a smart-ass toward Simon, you'd be on the highway with us," Greg suggested.

"Maybe I would."

"Have you seen Simon this morning?" Ben asked.

"Yep, he was here bright and early. That was an hour ago, and then he headed north," Ted replied.

"How'd that go?" Ben asked.

"He was decent enough," Bruce admitted.

"I tell you, the Sergeant's not that bad. Just meet him halfway, and things will go a lot smoother," Ben suggested. "He's got a job to do, too, just like we do."

"If you say so."

"I say so, too," Greg chimed in. "I've noticed he's loosened the reins with a lot of the guys over the past week."

"Not seeing that," Bruce snapped.

"Maybe because what goes around comes around. Try sugar instead of that sour-puss vinegar attitude."

"That's not in my nature," Bruce countered.

"Well, then I guess you make your bed. . ."


## Into a Hole

"We'd like to scout the French Quarter. Can you guys cover for us if we need it?" Ben asked.

"For you, anything," Bruce replied.

"Thanks. I knew you were a stand-up guy, especially after we explored that brick complex east of SP-16."

"I'm supportive of off-road adventures. I know patrol can get boring."

"It can, at times," Greg echoed.

"I haven't been anywhere yet," Ted interrupted. "My usual partner, Frank Succors, is a by-the-book guy. He's so straight-laced that he'd never venture out of the AO."

Greg's eyebrows lifted in surprise. "Oh, that's useful information. Guess I won't be talking to Succors about any of my off-the-road excursions."

"Not if you want to stay safe," Bruce suggested.

"Either way, the truth is that several patrols have already explored the French Quarter, and they've come back with great stories. There's serious business going on behind some of those high-walled villas," Ben added.

"Don't tell Succors. He'll want to conduct a search-and-arrest operation. He's one hard-core maniac," Ted cautioned.

"Charlie One, Charlie One, this is Papa Sierra One, over," the voice crackled over the radio.

Greg glanced at Ben. "That's Simon's call sign. I wonder where he's at."

Ben grabbed the mic and replied, "Papa Sierra One, this is Charlie One, over."

"Roger, Charlie One. What's your twenty, over?"

"Sierra Papa One One, over."

"How's the wind there? We're getting a lot of dust here," the voice asked.

"What the fuck!" Greg exclaimed to Ben. "That's our code for switching to an alternative frequency. How the hell does Simon know that?"

"That was Henry's voice. He's driving Simon today. I've worked with Holt; he's cool. But I don't know why he's using our emergency signal when he's with Simon. That's crazy."

Ben keyed the mic and replied, "Roger that. We're getting wind here."

Ben twisted one of the radio frequency dials, waited a minute, and keyed the mic twice to send a squelch. A double squelch came in response, and he knew they'd connected with Henry on the alternate frequency.

"You're received – go ahead," Ben stated.

"Long, we're in trouble," Henry replied.

"What's going on?"

"Can't say on the air. Can you find the blue gate?"

"Roger that."

"We need you here, and if you trust Bravo One, bring help."

"Roger and out."

The men stared at each other in disbelief.

"Is this what I think it is?" Bruce asked. "Our precious new Sergeant is out of the AO and in trouble?"

Greg looked puzzled, and Ted remained silent.

"Well, Holt drove Simon, so I know where they are. Their situation can't be good if they're using the alternate frequency to call for help," Ben replied.

"No shit," Greg echoed. "This is a mess. I know the guys on Bravo One. We can trust them. I'll call and get them on the alternate frequency to coordinate a rendezvous." He made the call and suggested a place for them to meet.

Ben turned to Bruce and Ted. "Well, here we go, wish us luck."

"Too bad we can't leave our post," Bruce replied half-heartedly. "I'd love to see Simon in a compromised situation."

"You're stuck here. Besides, there's no sense in all of us going into the French Quarter," Greg suggested.

Ben drove to the highway and turned north. Within a few minutes, he pulled onto the dirt road that passed through the French Quarter's perimeter wall. Once inside the shielded area, Ben waited until Bravo One arrived. The two patrols traveled to the villa with the massive blue gate, and Ben used the signal he learned from Henry. A large Chinese man eased the metal gate open and allowed the MP vehicles to enter the compound.

"Oh, shit!" Greg gasped.

"Holy fuck, this is bad!" Ben exclaimed when he saw the patrol sergeant's vehicle sunk halfway into a hole.

Greg carefully examined the scene. "The vehicle backed into an open well. It's stuck at an angle. Look, the front wheels can't get traction."

## All the King's Horses

"Maybe we can pull it out," Ben suggested. "Let's get some rope."

The men gathered ropes from the villa and tied tow lines to each patrol vehicle. Fifteen minutes of effort failed to dislodge the Sergeant's jeep.

"Damn, this fucking jeep's stuck in the hole but good!" Greg exclaimed.

"We don't have enough horsepower to pull the jeep out," Sergeant Simon declared.

"Maybe we can ask for help from those men inside?" Ben wondered.

"Papa Sierra One, Papa Sierra One, this is Papa Mike Oscar. What's your twenty?" the radio crackled.

Startled by the call, no one moved toward the radio.

"Charlie One, Charlie One, this is Papa Mike Oscar. What's your twenty?"

"That's that damn cherry PMO operator. He's looking for the patrol supervisor," Ben explained.

"Bravo One, Bravo One, this is Papa Mike Oscar. What's your twenty?"

"We're fucked," Greg announced in a tone of resignation.

"It's bad, that's for sure," Ben concurred.

"Papa Sierra One, Papa Sierra One, this is Papa Mike Oscar. I say again, what's your twenty?" the radio crackled.

Sergeant Simon looked at the men gathered around his vehicle. "This is on me. Thanks for trying to pull our ass out of that hole, but I think we all can see this situation's fucked."

The men mumbled in agreement, unsure what to do next.

"There's no sense in everybody going down for this FUBAR. You guys get back on patrol. I'll report the situation and request a wrecker."

"That'll be the kiss of death for you, Sarge," Greg declared.

"Can't be helped. We're out of time, and it doesn't look like we can get this jeep out of the hole."

The men grumbled about the unmarked well opening and the villa owners' irresponsibility for failing to put up a barrier.

"Nothing to do now but face the music. Get out while you still can."

"Charlie One, Charlie One, this is Lima Tango. What's your twenty?" the radio crackled.

"Shit, it sounds like the LT's on the road now. That asshole radio operator must have ratted us out to the officer on duty," Greg snarled.

Ben hurried to his vehicle, picked up the mic, and responded, "Lima Tango, Lima Tango, this is Charlie One. We're in the vicinity of Newport, over."

"We better get the fuck out of here," Greg insisted. "Sorry, Sergeant, we gotta split."

"You too, Bravo One. The jig's up. Everybody needs to get on the highway. Remember, you don't know anything about this situation," the Sergeant directed.

The MPs leaped into their vehicles and hurried out of the villa compound. Each patrol vehicle raced toward their sector. Ben drove south through the French Quarter on a dirt road that paralleled the highway. He turned east, passed through a separate opening in the perimeter wall, and turned south onto the four-lane pavement.

They listened as Sergeant Simon reported his location to the PMO and requested a wrecker.

"That'll draw the LT to the French Quarter, but it'll take him a while to find the right villa. We'll be in the clear in a few minutes," Greg asserted.

"I hope so, but I feel sorry for Simon and Holt," Ben added.

In minutes, Charlie One pulled alongside SP-11. They explained to Bruce and Ted what happened at the villa and asked them to back up their cover story.

"That incident will be the end of Sergeant Simon's platoon leader role," Ted replied.

"But I appreciate that he didn't take our patrol down with him," Greg added.

Bruce hesitated, then acknowledged, "Maybe I was too quick to judge him."

"Maybe we all misjudged him," Ben suggested, shaking his head in disappointment.

"I knew he was just a hard-ass as a front," Greg continued. "I always thought he was a good guy once you got to know him."

"Reminds me of our conversation a couple of weeks ago," Bruce chimed in. "We need to remember people sometimes wear disguises. I guess I mistook him for a lifer asshole when he was actually one of us."

"Sounds like a lesson we all should learn," Greg concluded.

Ben and the others stood in silence. *It's just like Henry said to me yesterday. Circumstances aren't always what they appear to be.*

# LESSONS: Truth and Trust

## April 30, 1970

### The Truth of Words

"A real shocker yesterday, wasn't it?" Randy DeMarco asked Ben, standing beside him at the sandbagged wall.

"I'm still stunned. This past month has been one surprise after another."

"I guess people aren't always who they say they are."

"It feels longer ago than four weeks when we heard our new Sergeants introduce themselves."

"They said a lot of convincing things, or so we thought."

"I didn't like everything I heard, but I believed them," Ben sighed.

"Truth and trust are fragile possessions!"

"I didn't realize how true that was. Now I'm beginning to doubt what I thought about a lot of things."

"How do you mean?" Randy asked.

"I grew up in the mid-west, and my parents raised me to believe in the integrity of our leaders' words. My dad admired President Eisenhower."

"He was widely respected in my neighborhood near Detroit, too."

"I grew up in a church community, and everyone shared the same belief that great leaders were honest," Ben declared.

"I was brought up in a Jesuit discipline; we held similar beliefs."

"Now we're in Vietnam because our leaders say this is how we defend our country. Communism is an evil threat, and if America doesn't stop the spread in Asia, our national security is at risk."

"We heard the same messages. First, the Red Scare was followed by the Cuban Missile Crisis and the Soviet Union's oppression in Eastern Europe. We were told the Communists would take away our freedom!"

"What I don't understand is the violence against our leaders. Some people believe President Kennedy's assassination was the work of evil forces that opposed his positions on Cuba and civil rights."

"I heard similar talk about Robert Kennedy's assassination. Some didn't like his views on civil rights and the Vietnam War. They were afraid he was surging to win the Democratic nomination," Randy added.

"I don't know what to believe anymore," Ben admitted, shaking his head.

"It's confusing to me too. There are disagreements about those as-sassinations. Some people believe those men were killed for speaking out. Their messages were a threat to powerful interests."

"So what's the truth about all this?"

"It's more than the Kennedy's! Martin Luther King advocated for social justice and challenged racism. Malcolm X was murdered for not backing down from speaking the truth about power," Randy posed.

"We're living in violent times!"

"And controversial times! There are strong opinions and intense emotions on each side."

"You know, I accepted the argument that America needed to fight the spread of Communism; however, my faith in our leaders has wavered in the last few years. There've been situations where they didn't show honesty or truth. I've started to wonder if maybe I've been too naïve in trusting they'll always speak truthfully and that their behavior will be consistent with what they claim."

"It's hard to know what to believe sometimes," Randy sympathized.

"Which brings us back to the dilemma about our Sergeants."

"I hear ya on that! The contrast between Rockwell's and Simon's words and actions left me puzzled too."

"This experience is worse for me than being puzzled! That contradiction has burned like acid in my stomach. I believed they were genuine when they expressed their intentions. I doubt my own judgment now. Maybe some reasons explain why they behaved contrary to what they declared, but I didn't see this coming," Ben confessed.

"I didn't realize the situation hit you that hard."

"I've lost my unquestioning faith and trust in leadership. I don't know if I can continue to accept a leader's words without question anymore."

## Trust is Lost

Randy paused and pondered that statement. "Maybe it will help to talk it through?"

"Sergeant Rockwell wanted us to think he was a friendly, easygoing leader. And I heard through the grapevine that he initially acted as if he was."

"Yeah, he started on the right foot with a friendly, laid-back style that appealed to the guys. The climate in that platoon was positive. Rockwell did what he said he'd do. He was lenient and practiced low-key enforcement. Guard mount was relaxed compared to Sergeant Simon's."

"That's what I heard too. Rockwell's men said he had a light touch; life was easygoing in their platoon. But his lenient style triggered resentment from guys in my platoon," Ben added.

"Let's stop right there and acknowledge his behavior *was* consistent with his words! He did what he said, so he was truthful," Randy insisted.

"Okay, I'll grant you that point. But when platoons operate with contrasting styles, it's a prescription for friction."

"Exactly the real problem! The CO heard rumblings about inconsistency and called Sergeant Rockwell into HQ for a leadership clarification talk."

"In Army parlance, you mean he got his ass chewed," Ben restated.

"Right, that's what I said. The men in his platoon rallied around him, and their support buoyed Rockwell's sense that his men saw him as a good leader. That was his first stumble because his focus was on being popular with his men instead of being responsive to the CO's concerns."

"I get your point!" Ben exclaimed. "You think he's a people pleaser who wanted to be liked by his men, so he continued his laid-back approach."

"Yes, his ego overrode his duty. Perhaps his college background undercut his ability to adapt to the Army culture. He might have recognized the men were playing him if he had more practical leadership experience. The men in his platoon were manipulating him and encouraged him to stick to his easygoing style," Randy explained.

"That sounds like a lesson to remember."

"No shit! Remember, the CO's primary responsibility is mission success through unit cohesion. The rumblings of resentment posed a threat to cohesion. He began to show up at guard mount and directed the Lieutenant to monitor behavior on the road. After a week of observations, the CO ordered Sergeant Rockwell back to HQ for another conversation."

"I don't think this story is going to turn out well."

"You don't have to be a rocket scientist to figure that out!" Randy laughed. "No one discussed the meeting, but stories have a way of circulating. The company clerk claimed he had the inside scoop and fed the grapevine, and then the rumor mill amplified those stories with details. Everyone was talking about Sergeant Rockwell getting another ass-chewing. He was said to have emerged red-faced from HQ, darted to his hooch, and didn't reappear for hours. His men were stunned by the rumors, but others smugly exaggerated the details, regaling in the punishment laid on the too-lenient Sergeant."

"I'll bet guys in my platoon were at the front of that parade," Ben crowed.

"Either way, the CO's message was received loud and clear. Sergeant Rockwell's tone at guard mount became stern. He started to monitor and address his men's behavior. Uniform violations were suddenly enforced rather than ignored or treated lightly. Discipline tightened up, and morale in the platoon plummeted to rock-bottom."

"That matches what I heard. Rockwell behaved the opposite of what he said he'd do!"

"Just be sure to get the moral of the story right! He didn't choose to go back on his word – he was driven there by the CO," Randy emphasized.

Ben paused to reflect on that point.

"And that sad state of affairs continued to its natural conclusion. The unit devolved from a relaxed team into a mob of cynics who constantly complained in the barracks and the EM Club. They carped that their Sergeant was a worse prick than Sergeant Simon ever threatened to be. They accused Rockwell of reneging on his word. Some labeled him a two-faced liar."

"Everyone in the company noticed those changes and heard men recounting Sergeant Rockwell's flaws," Ben affirmed.

"So let's dig into the lessons. Several problems undermined Rockwell's efforts to win the hearts and minds of his men, and ultimately led to his downfall."

Ben edged closer as if preparing to receive a sacrament.

"The first problem was the CO didn't support Rockwell's leadership style. Rockwell's words about leadership were suitable in a liberal college environment but not in the Army. The Commander directs a subordinate's leadership style, and Sergeant Rockwell's leadership style was a serious misstep. That misalignment from his superiors was Rockwell's first strike."

*Anyone who's been in the military for any length of time, or somebody like me who grew up in a military family, will know that rule – stay in line.*

Randy continued, "The second problem was Sergeant Rockwell's inability to maintain the respect and trust of his men. He received support at first because his words and actions afforded them a more comfortable life; however, he lost their confidence when his style changed from leniency to strict enforcement."

*I can relate to that! Men don't care about the reasons why somebody's behavior changes negatively. They feel betrayed, no longer trusting he is who he said he is, and chafe under his authority. I felt those feelings and emotions after dad changed from being friendly to an angry drunk man.*

"The men weren't overtly insubordinate, but it was evident the Sergeant's ability to lead was eroding. Loss of trust, respect, and compliance from his men would become strike two," Randy added.

"That's the kiss of death," Ben noted.

"The power of leadership rests on followers' trust in the leader's integrity and their willingness to accept authority. Trust is especially critical in the military. When Sergeant Rockwell lost his men's confidence, he lost his effectiveness. Morale and discipline rapidly deteriorated, and that jeopardized the success of the mission. The risk of the mission was the third strike."

"If men don't follow you, you aren't a leader," Ben declared.

"The CO heard about Rockwell's compromised ability to lead the platoon. He relieved him of duty and quietly transferred him out of the Company."

Ben reflected on those changes and the powerful lesson to be learned. *Be careful what promises you make and the expectations you set. When a leader doesn't follow through on his commitments, he sows the seeds of his downfall. He'll lose, first his honor as a trustworthy person and then his leadership position.*

## Poor Judgment

"There are different lessons from the other NCO," Randy asserted. "Sergeant Simon expressed a dramatically different message. He set a strict standard and declared he was a disciplinarian who expected everyone to follow his word as law. He threatened punishment for all uniform violations and misbehavior."

"*We* believed him and resigned ourselves to toe the line to his draconian rule. The platoon became a role model for military STRAC."

"He got everyone in shape immediately with that message, didn't he?"

"Yes, we didn't like Sergeant Simon's harsh discipline, But then we felt pride in our unit's professionalism. Simon surprised us when he generously complimented us on our appearance and performance. That balance of stringent demands and compliments was unexpected! The guys were caught off-guard by his kindness. A lot of them reconsidered their initial impression of him," Ben explained.

"I noticed another positive outcome. Within two weeks, the platoon had become STRAC, and the CO stopped attending guard mount."

"Our STRAC professionalism had another effect. Once we met his performance standards, we resented the inconsistency between platoons. We rejected Rockwell's casual standards, and some guys even mocked his platoon for their lackadaisical attitude."

"I bet that divisive climate didn't go unnoticed at HQ!"

"There's something else I can share about the Sergeant. When I served as Simon's driver, I gained an insight into the man behind the stripes. He explained how he wanted his leadership message to establish an aura of intimidation over the men, and he reinforced that message with threats of swift discipline. He learned that skill at his construction job back home and fine-tuned the method in his first months in-country." (See Story 64, Supervisor's Driver).

"So, you're saying he wasn't as bad as he sounded?"

"Not really! His hard exterior was a tactic to motivate the men. He called it leveraging first impressions."

Randy lifted his eyebrows in amazement. "Sounds like the same logic we use as MPs."

"And that tactic works! Showing excessive force to suppress resistance reduces the risk of harm to us."

"From what I saw, Sergeant Simon's style was effective in achieving his objective – to ensure the platoon would demonstrate excellence."

Ben nodded and gazed toward the sky. "Looking back, I realize he was pretty smart. He focused on meeting the CO's requirements and reasoned once he demonstrated effective leadership, his platoon would no longer be under scrutiny."

"Isn't that the same approach you take? I know some guys call you a suck-up but aren't you just playing the game so patrol supervisors think you're a STRAC MP and no longer think they have to keep an eye on you?"

"That's what I do. The lack of scrutiny allows opportunities for me to explore outside our AO," Ben crowed.

"I remember you mentioning some trips. You could enjoy those interesting excursions unless things went wrong!" Randy admonished.

Ben sighed and turned his gaze back to Randy. "There's always some risk when you take those chances. Unfortunately, that's what torpedoed Sergeant Simon in the French Quarter. When his driver backed into that open well, the shit hit the fan!"

"I heard the Lieutenant arrived at the scene and determined Sergeant Simon's behavior was inappropriate."

"That was bad timing! We could've solved the problem if we'd more time."

Randy paused and shook his head. "LT reported the incident to the CO, who relieved the Sergeant of duty."

"Yeah, that turned a bad situation into a disaster. Simon was a good leader; he just got caught in a difficult situation. I was sorry to see him transferred out of our Company."

## Lessons

Randy nodded and challenged, "Have you learned anything from that situation?".

"I sure have! First, I'd like to step back from that incident and re-cap some of the lessons I've learned about leadership."

"Whatever you want to say! I'm all ears."

"Well, Sergeant Simon's leadership style drove home a powerful lesson. Start with strict control and discipline to enforce early compliance. Once you've established order, you can loosen the reins and ease restrictions."

"It seems the guys responded positively, in the end, to the transition from harsh to easygoing," Randy replied.

"In the end is the key term, though. Nobody liked Simon at the start because he came off as a heavy-handed hard-ass."

"But, in the end, the men considered Sergeant Simon a nice guy and sympathized with his final circumstances. His reputation ended up being positive."

"That's true! We respected his style and felt like we learned from him."

"Any lessons on the other Sergeant, Rockwell?" Randy asked.

"Most of the guys thought Sergeant Rockwell was an ineffective leader and poor role model. Some thought he was a lying bastard who pretended to be friendly but then revealed his true colors as a punishing jerk."

"That's too harsh, don't you think? Wasn't he also a nice guy who got caught in the political battles over Army leadership culture?" Randy countered.

"I suppose that's true, to a degree, but the lingering effect of Rockwell has been negative. It doesn't matter whether the guys' perceptions are unfair or inaccurate – their anger toward his behavior change shaped their opinions. People generally dislike someone who initially makes them feel comfortable and later leaves them fearful and angry," Ben concluded.

"I'd agree that kind of change is hard to accept!" Randy excitedly replied.

The setting sun prompted them to walk toward the hooch as Ben asserted, "You know, my first month in this Company has been an eye-opener. I think this has been a better educational experience than anything I learned in college. Some points are still confusing, maybe even contradictory, but a few thoughts stand out for me about leadership."

Randy grew even more animated. "This should be interesting! I always want to hear what people learn from their experiences."

"Okay, now I know you're a smart ass!"

"No, seriously! I'd like to hear what you think."

Ben hesitated, still doubtful, but continued, "All right. My first thought is people are willing to believe their leaders and want to see them as honest."

"I'm with you on that! Like we already agreed on, most people hope and expect their leaders to be trustworthy and have integrity."

Ben nodded. "My second thought is leaders strive to sound sincere and want others to see them as genuine."

"But, as we experienced, leaders must behave consistently with their words to support that point of view," Randy cautioned.

"That turned out to undercut both Sergeants."

"We're on the same page again with that point."

"My third thought is more of a guess, but I'm wondering if underlying personal needs drive some leaders. For example, Sergeant Rockwell wanted to be well-liked, so he over-compensated to be a people pleaser. He focused on saying what he thought his men wanted to hear. On the other hand, Sergeant Simon wanted the latitude to do his own thing, free of direct oversight."

"That's an interesting thought. After all, people have personal histories, egos, and insecurities. I gotta believe that stuff influences their thinking and behavior somewhere along the line." Randy suggested.

"I know that stuff affects how I do MP work! Why wouldn't it impact how a leader approaches using his authority?"

"A ton of books could be written about that."

"So, along those same lines, I have a related fourth thought about the pattern in leaders' behavior. It might sound obvious, but external factors impact leaders' choices about action."

"Give me an example."

"Unexpected events can derail even the best of plans. Sergeant Rockwell's well-intended style ran aground on organizational politics. Sergeant Simon ran aground due to an unforeseen accident at an open well."

"Ah, the best-laid plans of mice and men!" Randy wistfully exclaimed.

"Well, aren't you the well-read man!" Ben laughed.

"I keep telling you a Jesuit education is the best in the world!"

Ben smirked at the remark and side-stepped to continue. "My fifth thought is the crux of everything we've discussed. When actions are inconsistent with words, trust is lost."

"Ah, yes, the pinnacle of truth! Even though we might forget everything else, we must hold tightly to this insight."

Ben stared in astonishment, unsure how to respond.

Randy studied Ben's puzzled expression. "Can't you see it? External factors and the reasons for inconsistency don't matter in the long run to those who believe a leader betrayed their trust."

Ben excitedly nodded, "Of course! So my final thought is about the consequence of lost trust. When trust is lost, followers are no longer willing to support their leader."

"Again, that is the kiss of death for a leader, something from which there is no recovery," Randy declared.

*I don't know if I'll ever be in a leadership role, but these lessons will be foremost in my mind if that happens.*

# Glossary

**AIT**: Army acronym for Advanced Individual Training; Military Occupation Service School

**AO:** area of operation, terrain assigned to specific units to maintain security

**Ao Dai**: ("owzeye") traditional Vietnamese slit dress with trousers

**Arty**: slang for artillery

**ARVN**: acronym for Army of the Republic of Vietnam, South Vietnamese soldiers

**Ba Mui Ba:** ("33") Vietnamese beer, rumored to be spiked with formaldehyde

**Beaucoup:** (French) can mean many, much, big, huge, very

**Betel Nut:** leaves or root of the betel palm, mildly narcotic. Chewed by many aged Vietnamese, especially women, to relieve the pain of diseased gums. Blackens the teeth_

**Bien Hoa**: 4th largest city in South Vietnam, 25 miles north of Saigon

**Blanket Party:** form of corporal punishment, administered by peers, to improve compliance with behavior expectations.

**Boom-boom:** Vietnamese slang for having sex with GIs

**Bouncing Betty:** a class of mines known as bounding mines; when triggered, mines launch into the air and detonate at waist height, spraying shrapnel in 360 degrees

**Boy-sans**: slang for young boys

**Butterfly**: Vietnamese slang for playboy.

**Cam on** ("cahm oon"): Vietnamese for "thank you."

**Canh Sat** ("cahn zaht"): Vietnamese National Police, nicknamed White Mice

**Cheap Charlie:** anyone, especially U.S. serviceman, who does not waste his money

**Cherry**: soldiers 'new' in-country who had not yet become versed in safety skills

**Con Biet:** Vietnamese for do you understand?

**Cowboy**: young Vietnamese male thugs who troll streets on motor bikes

**CPP**: Combined Police Patrols, six man units comprised of National Police (White Mice), QCs (Quan Shat are ARVN Military Police), and US Military Police

**Cyclo**: bicycle or motor scooter, with a bench seat in front for passengers

**DEROS:** acronym for 'date an employee is expected to return from overseas'; refers to soldier's end of tour of duty.

**Deuce-and-a-half:** two and one/half ton truck

**Di An Base Camp**: military base between Thu Duc and Bien Hoa

**Di di (mau)** ("dee-dee maow"): Vietnamese for "go away (fast) or "let's go (fast)"

**Dinky Dau:** slang for crazy or mentally incompetent

**Don't mean nothin':** coping expression indicating there's no problem, but infers this means everything and I could lose it. Used to dismiss experiences or events that are horrific, but are actually too much to acknowledge in the moment

**Dung lai:** ("zoong lye") Vietnamese for halt or stop

**Dong**: Vietnamese money

**ETS**: Army acronym for End Tour of Service

**Evac Choppers**: Huey helicopters marked with Red Cross, used to move wounded soldiers

**FNG**: acronym for 'fucking new guy' a derisive term for cherries

**Frag:** fragmentation grenade. Refers to retaliatory attack to injure or murder fellow soldiers. Typically done by tossing a grenade into a latrine or barracks occupied by target.

**Freedom bird:** aircraft which returns servicemen to the U.S.

**FUBAR**: military acronym from WW II, meaning Fucked Up Beyond Any Recognition

**Get Your Shit Together:** means to shape up and learn everything possible to stay alive

**Go Bags**: bag containing essential equipment, ammo and supplies solders take on a mission

**Greenbacks**: slang for U.S. paper currency, illegal to possess or exchange in Vietnam

**Heads:** group identified as dopers, those who use marijuana or heroin

**Hog /Pig:** nickname for the U.S. M-60 machine gun

**Hooch**: nickname for huts, or living quarters

**Incoming:** warning of impending aerial barrage of mortars, rockets, artillery

**In-country:** in Vietnam

**I shit you not:** GI slang meaning I am very serious

**Jody**: military culture reference to a man that stays home and steals the girl of a service man_

**Joint**: hand-rolled marijuana cigarette_

**Juicers:** group identified as beer and whiskey drinkers (alcohol)

**Lambretta**: small vehicle (8′ long) with covered driver cab and rear compartment of built-in parallel benches for transporting passengers (~ 10)

**Lai Day:** ("lye dye") Vietnamese for come here

**LBJ:** acronym for Long Binh Jail, the Army stockade at Long Binh Base

**Lifers:** career soldiers

**Lima Charlie:** phonetic alphabet words for LC, meaning loud and clear ~ radio parlance

**Lock and Load:** arm and ready your weapons

**Long Binh**: one of largest US bases in South Vietnam, 20 miles northeast of Saigon

**MACV:** acronym for Military Assistance Command, Vietnam, located at Tan Son Nhut Airport

**Mad Minute:** order given to fire across their field of fire for one minute, used as Recon by Fire in the field; used as slang to refer to an intense but brief firefight

**Mama San:** GI reference to older Vietnamese women

**Mau len:** ("maow len") Vietnamese for hurry up, go fast, or speed

**MIA:** acronym for Missing in Action, designation for GIs missing but not confirmed killed

**MOS:** acronym for military occupation specialty, the code for Army duty assignments

**MPC**: acronym for military paper certificates, script used as money by U.S. personnel_

**MPC**: Military Police Company, not to be confused with military paper certificates

**Namaste**: hand gesture frequently used for greeting among Buddhists

**Nha Be**: naval support base 5 miles downstream from Saigon on Song Nah Be River

**No Bic:** Vietnamese for I don't understand or speak your language

**No Sweat:** GI slang for a task that is easy or simple, indicates it will be done

**Numbah One GI:** Vietnamese slang for GIs who are viewed positive for spending money

**Numbah Ten GI:** Vietnamese slang for GIs who won't spend money, Cheap Charlie

**Numbah ten-thousand:** absolutely the worst

**Nuoc mam**: Vietnamese fish sauce of fermented fish and salt, has very pungent smell

**Papa San:** GI reference to older Vietnamese men

**Park Lane**: branded cigarettes that concealed marijuana joints, Vietnamese product

**Piastre**: Vietnamese paper currency, originally from French Indochinese usage

**Pomelo**: Vietnamese grapefruit

**Quan Cahn:** ("kwuhn kein") Vietnamese ARVN Military Police

**RA:** acronym for Regular Army; those who voluntarily joined the service

**REMFs:** acronym for rear-echelon mother fuckers, derogatory term used by combat troops referring to the non-combat troops safely at bases away from enemy contact

**Roach**: very small end of the remainder of a joint

**Round Eye:** Caucasian woman; contrasted to Asian women

**RPG:** acronym for Rocket-propelled Grenade; frequent weapon of VC /NVA

**Saigon Tea:** colored water or soda drink that a GI is asked to buy as the price for a hostess' company at a bar or nightclub

**Sappers**: soldiers specialized in sneaking through barbed wire with explosives into bases

**Shit Burning:** a 10-hour process where half-barrels of human waste are removed from latrines and burned using a kerosene and diesel fuel mixture, continuously stirred to burn all the waste

**Short:** slang meaning an individual's tour of duty is nearly completed; less than 100 days.

**Sit Rep:** Situation Report – posts are contacted to report their status, usually hourly

**SNAFU:** acronym for Situation Normal, All Fucked Up

**Sorry 'bout that**: mocking or sarcastic apology

**Spider Hole**: camouflaged foxhole, designed for observation, or attack

**Squared Away:** neat, orderly, organized

**Strac:** military acronym meaning militarily precise in both dress and skill

**Tan Son Nhut** : air base on western edge of Saigon in South Vietnam

**The World:** GI slang for the U.S.A.; as in asking where are you from back-in-the-world?

**Thu Duc:** town 7 miles north of Saigon, situated on QL-1

**Ti Ti:** ("tee tee") Vietnamese for very small, or short

**US:** classification assigned to soldiers who were drafted

**V:** V-100 armored car, manufactured by Cadillac, used for convoy escort

**Wasted:** multiple meanings ~ high on drugs, drunk from booze, unable to function, or dead

**White Mice**: nickname for National Police based on small stature and white shirt uniforms

**Xin Loi**: ("sin loyee") Vietnamese for "pardon me", or sarcastic "sorry about that" or "tough shit"

# Author Biography

Ben Thieu Long (pseudonym) is publishing his memoir after a forty-year human resources career in manufacturing, higher education and healthcare. He successfully led organizational change and coached individuals to navigate difficult circumstances and rebound as stronger and healthier people.

Ben's life lesson is that although people sometimes don't select the best path or make wise choices, they can learn from experience and achieve future success. He attributes his military experience for his personal courage to persist in the face of adversity, his professional success, and his personal resilience when confronted by challenging circumstances.

Ben's *13 Moons* series fulfills a commitment he made during his tour of duty in Vietnam, where he served as a US Army military policeman. He faced multiple temptations and moral contradictions, and an examination of his behavior led him to question his commitment to his values and faith. Those experiences reshaped his perspective on courage, moral strength, and resilience as he learned lessons that guided him positively through his life's challenges.

CPSIA information can be obtained
at www.ICGtesting.com
Printed in the USA
BVHW031224150521
607358BV00006B/470